JACOB'S JACKPOT

Sunsets and Saddles Book 3

MICHELE LINDSEY

Jacob's Jackpot

Sunsets and Saddles Book 3

Michele Lindsey

Introduction

When Jacob's bad luck at the poker table nearly gets him shot, a familiar face comes to the rescue and offers to pay his debt. The only condition: Jacob must work at the fancy Colorado Springs Grand Hotel to repay that debt.

The last thing New York socialite Mathilda Coventry wants to do is travel to Colorado to marry a man she's never met. But it's an arrangement she can't get out of. And to make matters worse, Tillie's first meeting with her betrothed is a disaster.

Then she meets Jacob. And while he can't offer her the life she's used to, he has the ability to give her the only thing she truly wants … love. But how can she break free from the man she's supposed to marry? Especially when there's more to the arrangement than meets the eye—something that might just get Tillie or Jacob killed.

Chapter One

Wednesday, 3:35 p.m.

The dimly lit saloon was a good place to be during the hottest part of the day. This was something ranch hand, Jacob Smithers, had only recently come to realize. Although it was the game of poker that drove him there. And that too, was fairly new to him.

But he'd caught the bug.

Maybe it was the challenge of honing a new skill or the thrill of the bluff, either way Jacob found it exciting to be sitting amongst the toughest of the tough, playing cards and shooting back whiskeys. It made him feel more like a man. Even though they called him "Kid."

Jacob may have been the youngest one at the table, but he was no kid. Either way, *this kid* was feeling lucky. He spread the cards in his hands, so each corner was visible: four aces and a joker. The toe of his boot tapped silently under the table as he eyed the pile of cash in the center. That jackpot was as good as his. But he had to keep his cool. He couldn't let on how confident he was—didn't want the others to fold.

With his mouth going dry, Jacob wanted to take a swig of his drink. But he didn't dare. After the last few weeks playing and observing, he'd picked up on easy tells. That could be anything from finger tapping, fidgeting, or even taking a drink. The fellow sitting to the left of the dealer, the one with the toothpick hanging out of his mouth, Gantz, would flip the toothpick around and start chomping on the dry end when he was nervous. And to Jacob's right, was Curly. He would twist the ends of his mustache between his fingers when he liked his hand.

To Jacob's left sat Two-Shot Shirley, a bead of sweat forming at his temple.

The dealer eyed him. "What's it gonna be?"

Two-Shot stared down at his cards fanned in his hands and swallowed hard, his Adam's apple bobbing up and down. Then with a huff, he slid the fan closed and slapped them face down. "I'm out."

All eyes moved to the one they called The Boss. He was the only one at the table to remove his hat and the only one Jacob hadn't been able to crack yet. The man never engaged in conversation and he always looked angry. Even when he was winning. And unlike the other men with their callused hands and thick, weathered skin, layered with sweat and prairie dust, The Boss looked as though he'd never truly worked a day in his life.

"I'm in, an' I'll raise it twenty," The Boss said as he tossed several bills onto the pile.

Jacob's stomach dropped.

"Twenty!" Gantz repeated with irritation before flipping the toothpick with his tongue. "I thought the limit was five?"

"Well I'm raisin' it," The Boss said in a deep, foreboding voice, moving his hand slowly towards his leather holster. "Anyone here got a problem with that?" His gaze scanned the players at the table, as if daring someone to oppose.

Gantz leaned back in his seat, indicating he didn't want any trouble. "Too rich for me," he said gently tossing his cards face down.

Next up was Curly. He studied his cards, flicking the corners with his thumbnail. The fact that his fingers weren't on his mustache, told Jacob that the man was about to fold.

After a tense, quiet minute, Curly slapped his cards face down in frustration. "Yeah, I fold."

Nerves rumbled through Jacob's body as all eyes turned on him. It was down to just himself and The Boss. And while he knew he had the hand to win, he did not have the money to cover the wager.

Jacob swallowed hard. He looked down at his dwindling stash. "Uh, I don't have enough on me to see yer raise, but—"

The Boss cut him off. "Ya feeling lucky, Kid?"

Jacob's eyes flashed to those four beautiful aces. "I think so," he answered casually.

"Are you good for it?" The Boss asked regarding Jacob's ability to pay if he lost.

"Why yes," Jacob lied. Even though he knew he didn't have anything of value he could offer. But in his eyes, it wouldn't matter because there was no way he could lose. And therefore, they'd never know.

"Well then let's see whatcha got," The Boss said, obviously taking Jacob's bet.

Jacob's heart pounded hard in his chest. He couldn't believe such a lucky hand had been dealt to him. He slowly spread his cards out on the table. "Joker's wild," he replied.

The room went silent.

Jacob couldn't breathe. He felt like he could cut the tension with a knife. Like, suddenly he'd made a big mistake going up against a man like The Boss, who by the way had two of his own bodyguards sitting nearby. And they, like The Boss, were the kind of men who wore six-shooters on their hips and wouldn't think twice before pulling one out and cocking the hammer. If you were lucky —and Jacob hoped that he was—they'd keep their finger off the hair trigger.

The Boss placed a king of diamonds on the table, then the queen. He made a *tsk* sound with his tongue before sucking in a breath and leveling his stare. "Now d'you wanna tell me," he began, laying down the jack and ten, "how it is that we both have an ace of diamonds?" he asked as he dropped the ace in front of the king.

Jacob felt a cold wave rush through his body. A royal flush was an excellent hand. However, it didn't beat his five of a kind. Although the fact that there should only be four aces sitting on the table right now meant that someone cheated. And even though Jacob could swear on the bible that it wasn't him, he figured at this particular juncture it didn't matter one bit. He knew he was rightfully screwed.

The Boss looked up at one of his bodyguards and gave a nod. With that, the two hired guns moved in.

"Whoa! Whoa! Whoa!" Jacob shouted from his seat, holding out his arms in defense. He saw his life flash before his eyes as the two men grabbed him by the arms.

His chair fell with a bang as they pulled him backwards, over the fallen chair and straight out the door. He tried to scramble to his feet but couldn't make purchase in his current precarious position.

The heels of his boots clunked noisily as they dragged him down the wooden steps to hard-packed street below.

The men swung him around like a ragdoll and when he finally got his bearings, it was just in time to see the large fist before it made contact with his face. The blow had him seeing stars and going limp in the knees. But they wouldn't let him fall. They weren't done with him yet.

As the larger, smellier of the two men drew his arm back to deliver another punch, a shout rang out.

"What's going on here?"

The man lowered his fist and turned.

"And who're you to be askin' 'bout our business?" asked the man who held Jacob's arms behind his back.

"I'm Edgar Salzman. I know this boy and if he's in some kind of trouble I'd like to offer assistance."

The larger man hitched his chin, looking the finely dressed man over. "What kinda assistance you talkin' 'bout?"

"Why don't you first tell me what this boy's done to deserve such a licking," Mr. Salzman answered, hooking his thumbs in the armholes of his vest, and rocking back on his heels.

"He's a cheater," the smaller, red-haired man answered, still pinning Jacob in place.

"I didn't cheat, I swear," Jacob said twisting his neck to look the guy in the eye. "Please, ya gotta listen to me."

The larger man glared and lifted his fist again. "Are you implyin' The Boss is a cheater?"

"No!" Jacob answered, pressing himself closer to the man holding him, in an attempt to put distance between his face and the man's fist. "No, no, that's not what I'm saying. I think there's just been some kinda misunderstanding is all."

Mr. Salzman stepped closer and reached into his pocket. "How much is it going to cost to set things right with this here boy and your boss?"

Jacob's captor loosened his grip. "I'd say a hundred oughta do it."

Chin to shoulder, Jacob tried to eye the man again. "But that's five times the wager!"

"The extra is for upsettin' The Boss."

Mr. Salzman pulled some folded bills from his pocket, slipped a few free and held them out. "How about I give you fifty and we'll call it even. What do you say?"

Eyes wide, Jacob held his breath as the thugs passed a glance between them.

"What da ya think?" the red-haired man asked his partner.

The larger man answered with a stiff nod, then stepped forward and swiped the money from Mr. Salzman's hand. "He's all yours."

The red-haired man shoved Jacob, freeing him. "Nice doin' business with ya," he said tipping his hat.

Jacob sighed in relief and picked his hat up off the ground. Putting a hand to his jaw, he looked up at his savior, Mr. Salzman. The man owned a fancy new hotel in Colorado Springs, and he was a friend of the ranch owners where Jacob lived and worked.

"Thank you, sir. I'll need some time to come up with the money, but I promise I'll find a way to pay you back."

Calmly, the hotel owner stuffed the remaining bills in his pocket. "Does Nathaniel Price, know about the gambling?"

"Uhh … no, sir."

"What do you think he'd say if he knew you were hanging out with the likes of these people—gambling and fighting?" The man raised his nose in the air and took a whiff. "Smells like you've been drinking too," he added.

A lump formed in Jacob's throat. Nathaniel was more than an employer to Jacob, he'd been like a father to him.

And the last thing Jacob wanted to do was disappoint the man.

"I'd rather he not find out." Jacob held his hat in front of him with both hands, nervously clenching and curling the rim.

The older gentleman looked Jacob over and thought a moment. "Come to the Grand Hotel at three tomorrow. Make sure you clean yourself up first—don't come dirty and sweaty from your ranchin' work."

Jacob's eyes narrowed. "I don't understand."

"If you got time to come all the way to Colorado City to gamble in the afternoons then you got time to come work for me in order to pay your debt." Before Jacob could respond, Mr. Salzman was on his way. "Good day," he called over his shoulder. "Three o'clock. Don't be late!"

———

"Tillie, honey, please put down the book and eat some lunch."

Tillie ignored her mother and flipped the page. It wasn't that she was so engrossed in her book that she couldn't stop to eat. Or that she had even finished reading the page she was on before turning to the next. The fact was, she'd already read Little Women once before and she was trying to make a point. And the point was that she didn't want to leave New York, she didn't want to be on this train, and she sure as heck didn't want to marry Harold Declan McAllister III.

"Mathilda," her father said with a harsh tone. "I don't know what you're hoping to accomplish by starving yourself, but I've just about had it. Now stop acting like a child and eat your dang sandwich."

Tillie eyed her father over the top of her book, then

snapped it closed. With her brow pinched and her mouth in a tight pucker, she swiped half the sandwich off the plate and took an exaggerated bite.

"Happy now?" she asked as she chewed.

Angry, her father looked away.

Seeing anguish in her mother's eyes and down-turned mouth, Tillie lifted her napkin to her lips and chewed softer, her eyes shifting down in shame. Why must her father push her all the time?

"We should be pulling into Colorado Springs around this time tomorrow," her mother said. "I'm sure we'll all feel better after a bath and a good night's sleep."

After six days in close quarters with her parents it was going to take a lot more than that. Like perhaps calling off the wedding and not forcing her to marry a man she didn't know.

Even though her stomach roiled, Tillie forced the sandwich down. Then, getting up from her seat, she excused herself. "I need to stretch my legs."

She opened the pocket door of their private sleeper car and stepped out, placing one hand on the wall opposite to steady herself. Her hand skated over the polished wood as she headed toward the rear of the train. The moving box of steel left her with little to no options of escape, so she headed toward the only place that would offer a few moments of absolute privacy. The lavatory.

Eventually, Tillie made her way back to her section. As she approached from behind, she heard her father's voice and stopped to listen.

"She's just so spoiled, Dorothy. You can't continue to coddle her," he said. Tillie's chest tightened.

"I know, but—"

"No buts," he interjected. "It's about time she grew up. She's nineteen, for God's sake."

Her mother sighed. "I just wish she didn't have to move so far away."

"I know, but that's the way it worked out," he answered. "Harry is hoping after his son is married and starting a family, he will realize he's had enough of the west and move back to New York. Look," he said with a sigh, "this is going to be a really good thing for her. Trust me."

"It's all just happening too fast," her mother griped. "We don't know him … and we're just supposed to hand our daughter over to him."

"I've known Harry McAllister for many years. He's an upstanding member of the community and a great businessman. I expect no less from any son of his." Lowering his voice, her father added, "And if all goes well, this is an arrangement that will work out in *everyone's* interest."

Tillie took a deep breath and rounded the corner, entering their section and taking her seat.

Her father quieted.

Her mother went back to her needlepoint, pulling the wooden loop from her carpet bag and punching the needle through the stretched fabric with precision and ease.

Tillie leaned her head and shoulder against the window and stared out at the Kansas landscape. Her father's words played over in her head as she watched mile after mile of flat, barren land pass her by.

He had said the arrangement would work out in everyone's interest.

But what about *her* interest?

A salty tear landed on her lips.

Why does everyone else get to decide my future?

Chapter Two

Thursday, 2:00 p.m.

The next day, after more than eight hours work on the ranch, Jacob cleaned himself up and headed out for the Grand Hotel.

The newly constructed hotel was the finest south Denver and was quickly attracting rich tourists to the growing town of Colorado Springs. A far cry from the neighboring town of Colorado City, which catered more to transients and miners, with their saloons full of drunk rowdies and painted ladies.

After tying his horse off at one of the posts in front, he approached the steps and looked up at the imposing, three-story building. Of course, he'd passed by the Grand Hotel before—many times, in fact—but he'd never had reason to go inside.

He found himself rather nervous.

Blowing out a cleansing breath, he clamored up the stairs.

Jacob stepped through the door at 3:01. He knew that

because Mr. Salzman was waiting just inside, with his pocket watch in his hand.

"You're a minute late," the man said, before tucking the watch away. "Take the hat off when you're inside my hotel. This is a respectable place."

"Yessir." Jacob quickly removed his hat and Mr. Salzman looked him over.

With a nod of approval, one side of his mouth curled. "You clean up nicely."

"Thank you, sir," Jacob answered. "And I just want you to know, I didn't cheat. I swear it."

"All right," the man answered with a nod. Jacob couldn't tell if Mr. Salzman believed him.

But he found himself distracted by the beauty and awe of his surroundings. Mouth agape, Jacob wandered further into the hotel.

The front lobby was a large, open area with massive columns going from the marble floors all the way to the incredibly tall ceilings. Directly across from the main entrance was the widest, grandest staircase Jacob had ever seen. To the right of the door sat the front desk with its marble countertop and beautifully polished wood-panel front.

He turned to take in the rest. Everywhere he looked he saw ornate woodwork, imported rugs, and crystal chandeliers, it was the epitome of luxurious. At the opposite end of the room was an enormous stone fireplace. Groupings of chairs and settees dotted the area, where several guests sat around chatting and laughing.

"First order of business," Mr. Salzman finally said, grabbing Jacob's attention. "I need you to take the hotel coach to the railroad station to pick up the Coventry family. It'll be the mister and missus and their daughter, coming all the way from New York City. They're coming in on the 3:15 train, so get a move on."

"Yessir." And with that, Jacob was off again.

Repeating the name Coventry in his head, Jacob stepped onto the platform just as the train was pulling in. He watched the passengers disembark. Many seemed to be traveling alone. There were a few women traveling together, and several couples. Finally, a man and woman stepped off, the woman held a small child's hand.

"Mr. Coventry," Jacob called out. Maybe the man didn't hear him. He called out again, louder this time, "I'm here for the Coventry family."

"I'm Theodore Coventry," a different man answered.

Following the voice, Jacob turned to see the man waving him over. He was talking to a porter, his wife stood beside them. But no child.

Jacob hustled over. "Welcome to Colorado Springs, sir. I'm here to help with your baggage."

"Great, great. I just gave this fine porter our baggage tickets," Mr. Coventry said. Jacob and the porter acknowledged each other with a nod. "After all that traveling, we'd like to walk. Please see that our bags are delivered to the Grand in a timely manner."

"You got it, sir."

Mrs. Coventry hooked her husband's arm and looked over her shoulder. "Tillie, dear," she sang out. "Come along, we're walking to the hotel."

A young woman sitting on a bench against the building —the only shady spot on the platform—got to her feet and opened her parasol. Jacob had seen fancy ladies before, but Tillie was to beat all. She wore an extravagant hat and matching dress with touches of ruffles and lace and a bustle that accentuated her tiny waist. And with her big, blue-gray eyes, her heart-shaped lips and perfect complexion, she looked like one of those porcelain dolls he'd seen on the top shelf at the mercantile.

Jacob watched as she joined her parents, left the platform, and disappeared around the corner.

After a couple of minutes of staring off, Jacob scanned for the porter that Mr. Coventry had given his tickets to. He spotted him down the line, stacking bags, boxes, and trunks on the platform.

"Well, gosh darnit, it's gonna take all day if I have to wait for him to unload the whole dang train," he groaned to himself as he headed over to the porter. "How am I supposed to find the Coventry's baggage in all this?" he asked with slight irritation.

The porter's gaze met Jacob's. "This *is* all the Coventry's baggage."

Jacob's mouth fell open. His shoulders slumped.

It took him a while, but Jacob managed to load it all up onto the back of the open stagecoach: four trunks, three wooden boxes marked fragile, and five heavy bags. At least when he got back to the hotel, he was able to rustle up some help from the bellhop. Still, it took them each four trips to get it all up to the second floor.

Since the family had reserved two adjoining rooms, Mrs. Coventry stood in the hallway, directing Jacob and the bellhop, Alvin, where to put everything. A small number of the bags went to the parents' room, but the majority went next door to their daughter's. She had the last room on the left.

Each room was the size of the house Jacob had grown up in. The walls were covered in fancy wallpaper in jewel tones of deep blue, red, and green, with gold accents. The rooms were nearly identical, each had a double bed with brass headboard, topped with luxurious linens. A Tiffany lamp stood atop the nightstand and a gilded mirror hung above a small chest of drawers. Across the room, a small pedestal table with two chairs and a settee filled the area in front of the large window which overlooked the mountains. And in one corner stood a tri-fold silk screen for modesty.

The daughter sat in a chair by the window as Jacob and Alvin came and went, delivering her things. She never once spoke, or smiled, or even made eye contact with either of the young men.

"And that one makes twelve. Great, they all made it," Mrs. Coventry said as Jacob approached with the last wooden box. "Be very careful with that one, it's my mother's china. She brought it all the way from England back in the fifties. It's very delicate," she added, leading the way. "Oh heavens, we're running out of room, uh … how about you put it over there."

"Alrighty." Jacob placed the box on top of one of the trunks and wiped his sweaty brow with the back of his hand.

"Could you pop the lid off that before you leave? I want to be sure it's still all in one piece."

The box had been nailed shut.

"Sure ma'am." Jacob pulled his trusty Barlow pocketknife from his pocket and worked around all four sides, to pry the top off.

As he did, Mrs. Coventry commented, "We're here for my daughter's wedding."

"Is that so?" Jacob replied with a smile as he set the lid to the side.

Mrs. Coventry pulled a plate from the wood shavings, held it up, and smiled. "Isn't it beautiful?"

"Yes, it is," Jacob answered politely. Although, he thought it was a little extravagant for his taste. It surely cost a fortune. And what was the point when you're just going to cover it up with food anyway?

"My mother handed them down to me and now I'm handing them down to my Tillie." She glanced back at her daughter, who quickly looked away. Mrs. Coventry faced Jacob again, her eyes shifting awkwardly. "Well, uh … thank you for all your help," she said holding her closed hand out.

Confused, Jacob extended his hand, palm up, and the woman dropped in two gold coins. His eyes flashed to hers. "Well, thank you, ma'am," he said with a smile. Then looking the daughter's way again, he said, "And best wishes on the weddin' miss." With no response from her, Jacob gave a nod to Mrs. Coventry and showed himself out.

He was barely out of sight when he heard the daughter speak for the first time.

"Why are you talking to the help, mother? They don't need to know our business."

Jacob shook his head and walked away. That daughter of theirs may be the most beautiful woman he'd ever seen, but she had the personality of a doorknob.

———

"HAVE YOU FORGOTTEN YOUR MANNERS?" Tillie's mother barked. "You couldn't have been colder to that gentleman if you tried. A simple thank you for bringing half of Manhattan up to your room would've been nice. Honestly," she huffed, "I don't know what's gotten into you?"

Tillie just didn't like her mother flaunting that she was getting married as if she was happy about it. She opened her mouth to speak, but her father walked in, cutting her off.

"Edgar Salzman, the hotel owner, has extended to us, an invitation to join his table for dinner tonight," he said.

"That was very kind," her mother replied with a smile, before passing a sideways glance at Tillie.

Tillie knew that look. It meant she was supposed to smile and act as if everything were swell. With pressed lips, the corners of her mouth curled in an attempt to appease.

"Very kind of him indeed," Tillie said politely. "You two enjoy your dinner. I'd like to get settled and relax in my room this evening—maybe have a small bite sent up later."

"There'll be plenty of time to get settled tomorrow." He waved his finger, indicating for her to move from the chair. "Now get changed. We need to head down to the dining room in about a half an hour." He turned to leave.

Tillie stood. "But Daddy—"

He tossed a look back to her.

"Put on something nice, we'll be meeting important people," he said with an air of finality as he left the room. From around the corner, he called out, "Dorothy, I'm going to need help finding a clean suit in all this mess."

"I'm coming, dear," her mother said sheepishly as she followed.

Alone, Tillie let the tears fall.

Put on something nice, she repeated in her head. Just sit there and look pretty—that's all anyone ever expected of her. She was so tired of being treated like a child. Always told what to do, what to wear, and even who to marry.

As Tillie removed her hat and stripped down to her undergarments, she caught a glimpse in the mirror over the wash basin. "Simply dreadful," she said to her reflection.

She wondered if thirty minutes would be enough time to make herself look presentable.

After washing up, Tillie unpinned her hair, letting it fall around her shoulders. She slapped some powder on it and gave it a good brushing. What she really needed was a bath.

With her hair slicked back in a chignon, it was time to find something to wear.

In a matter of minutes, her room looked as if it had been hit by a storm. She'd opened and rifled through two of her trunks—the latch on the third was stuck. Over a dozen dresses to choose from but she couldn't decide.

Finally, she settled on a green velvet dress. It was the least wrinkled.

She was slipping into it as her mother entered the room.

"Are you almost ready?" she asked.

"Yes," Tillie answered from behind the folding screen.

A moment later, she stepped out, smoothing and adjusting her skirt. She turned, wanting help with the back.

"You look beautiful," her mother said, working the last button.

Tillie ignored the compliment, grabbed her beaded reticule, and headed for the door. "Let's get this over with."

Chapter Three

Thursday, 4:30 p.m.

After helping the Coventrys, Mr. Salzman had Jacob assist in the kitchen as they were short-handed. With nearly every room in the hotel full and Mr. Salzman deciding to host a last-minute dinner party, he expected the kitchen to be busy.

Jacob's current mission: carry in a fifty-pound bag of potatoes and start peeling.

He'd been at it for a while, when Jeremiah, the kitchen manager came to him with a new job.

"Grab a clean apron and a pitcher of water and check on the Salzman's table. His guests are arriving."

"But I'm not a waiter." Jacob panicked.

"Can you pour a glass of water?"

"Yeah." He shrugged.

"Then go," Jeremiah ordered.

With pitcher in hand, Jacob pushed through the swinging door. The dining room was broken up into two spaces. The larger, main room extended toward the front of the building; it held about ten square-top tables with seating for four. The chairs were upholstered, and the tables covered with brilliant white linen tablecloths. And with the fancy china, crystal glassware, and polished silver, it was nothing like any other restaurant around.

Jacob spotted Mr. Salzman beyond the double doors, in the smaller room toward the back. That room had two square-tops and one long table that could probably seat up to ten. The hotel owner stood at the head of the long table, a woman by his side, greeting an older couple.

Jacob watched from several feet away, waiting to get some kind of sign from Mr. Salzman that he should approach. He'd never even been in a place like this before, let alone worked in one. He had no idea of etiquette and didn't want to embarrass himself or Mr. Salzman.

As the older couple began to take their seats, Mr. Salzman held up a finger, indicating to Jacob "not just yet."

Jacob nodded, staying back. He looked around at the quickly filling larger dining room, at the men and women dressed to the nines. At one table, he watched as a man pulled the chair out for the lady and waiter stood nearby. Just like Jacob, he wore a crisp white apron at his waist and held a pitcher.

Jacob mimicked the waiter's stance: standing tall and stiff, straight face, eyes looking forward, and his empty hand tucked behind his back. He felt like a statue. Like someone who was supposed to blend into the background and not be noticed. Which was fine by him since he felt like a fraud just being in the same room with the likes of these people.

Facing Mr. Salzman and his table again, Jacob waited for a sign.

Mr. Salzman extended his hand as another man

walked up. Jacob recognized him. It was Mr. Coventry. And following a short distance behind was the man's wife and daughter.

After greeting the Coventrys, everyone took their seats and Mr. Salzman finally gave the sign.

Jacob moved in, starting at the guest opposite the hotel owner. He had noticed the other waiter would pick up the glass before filling it, so Jacob did the same. He flashed a glance to Mr. Salzman who smiled and winked, assuring Jacob he was pleased.

He moved slowly around the table, distracted by the conversation and the fact that Tillie Coventry had yet to look up. The young woman seemed only interested in the place setting in front of her or her hands in her lap.

"This is my dear lady friend, Mavis Mumford," Mr. Salzman said, introducing the woman to his right, before going counterclockwise around the table and making the rest of the introductions. "Mr. Greenburg here, is in the tobacco business down in South Carolina. He and the missus arrived yesterday."

The Greenburgs were met with smiles and nods.

"What do you think of Colorado Springs so far?" Ms. Mumford asked.

"We do a lotta travelin' and I gotta say, this is one of the prettiest places we've evah been," Mr. Greenburg answered with a thick southern drawl.

Mrs. Greenburg agreed, "Absolutely the prettiest."

Mr. Salzman gestured toward the next guest, the one sitting directly across from him. "Everyone, this is Steven Hawthorn. I brought him in from Chicago. He's done brilliant work in marketing and with the tourism growing in the Springs and the opening of the Grand Hotel, he's going to help us spread the word. People from all over

America will want to visit—heck, maybe even the world," he ended with a hardy guffaw.

"That's our goal," Mr. Hawthorn boasted. He looked around the table. "Hello. Nice to meet you all."

Mr. Salzman turned to his left, slapping a hand on Mr. Coventry's shoulder. "And here we have Theodore Coventry." Jacob reached in from the right, grabbing and filling the hotel owner's glass as he spoke. "Theodore, and his wife and daughter, just arrived this afternoon—all the way from New York City."

"That's right. And please, call me Teddy," Mr. Coventry said with a huge grin. "This is a beautiful establishment you have here, Edgar. Thank you for having us."

Jacob could tell the man was influential. His voice was loud and bold, and he seemed to be the kind who did everything in a big way. This was a man who was used to being seen. And he reveled in it.

Jacob held back, not wanting to reach around him while he was talking.

"We're here for a wedding," he said, turning his smile to his daughter, sitting next to him. She raised her eyes for the first time. "My daughter Mathilda is getting married in five days. We'll be celebrating right here in this dining room and you're all invited."

While Jacob saw happiness in the proud father's eyes, he saw nothing of the sort in the eyes of the bride-to-be. Even when the other guests at the table began offering their blessings.

"May you have a happy and healthy life together," Mrs. Greenburg said as Jacob poured Mr. Coventry's water.

Mr. Greenburg raised his glass.

"Best wishes to the young couple," Ms. Mumford said.

Jacob returned the water glass to the table. In quick

order, the man reached for it and glanced up at Jacob, standing over his shoulder. "Thank you, son." Then he lifted the glass in the air. "Here! Here!

"He's a lucky man," Mr. Hawthorn replied, smiling and lifting his glass as he turned his gaze to Coventry's daughter.

Jacob moved to Mathilda, or Tillie as they tended to call her. He picked up her glass and began to pour.

"Why?" Tillie asked Mr. Hawthorn boldly.

Mr. Hawthorn lowered his glass, eyes wide. "Uh, why what?"

"Why do you say he's a lucky man?" she asked very matter of fact.

"Uh, I," he stuttered.

Mrs. Coventry tucked her chin to her shoulder—the one closest to her daughter—and spoke under her breath, "What are you doing?"

Tillie flashed a look to her mother, then back to Mr. Hawthorn. "I'm just curious. The way you looked at me, you implied that by marrying me, Declan McAllister is a lucky man. So, I'd like to know how you've come to such a conclusion when you know absolutely nothing about me, other than the way I look."

A snort escaped and Jacob fumbled as he went to set her glass back down. A bit spilled onto the tablecloth. "I'm so sorry," he said quietly.

He was both shocked and captivated by her gumption.

TILLIE LEANED AWAY from the clumsy waiter and looked up. Their eyes met. It was the young man who had brought their baggage to their room. For a moment, she was caught in his stare. His crystal blue eyes held a sparkle.

Pulling her focus away, her gaze scanned the guests at the table. She felt them all judging her for speaking out.

"Excuse me," Tillie said, throwing her napkin down and sliding her chair back. "I think I need some fresh air."

Everyone remained painfully quiet as she left the table. She was no more than two steps away when her father cleared his throat.

"Please excuse my daughter," he said. "She's just not herself right now, what with all the traveling and wedding jitters."

"That's women for ya," one of the men replied, setting off a round of laughter.

Tillie kept her eyes forward and walked faster, the tension building in her chest.

A bellhop standing near the front entrance saw her coming and rushed to open the door for her. "Good day, Miss."

"Good day," she responded with a firm nod, as she marched ahead. She thought about continuing down the steps, straight to the train station, and hopping the next train out of here.

But frankly, that wasn't an option.

Right now, she just needed a break from everyone, including her parents.

White rocking chairs and potted flowers dotted the raised, covered porch which spanned the front of the hotel. Tillie walked all the way to the end and sat down. Lowering her head, she closed her eyes and pulled a long breath in through her nose. Willing herself not to cry, she blew the breath slowly between her lips. She did that several times as her mind raced. In through her nose and out the mouth.

How did she get to this place in her life?

A month ago, she was happy. She had her friends. She

was working on a charity event committee to raise funds to help improve the children's wing at Bellevue and she had her eye on a boy from uptown. Oliver. Just the sight of him made her heart flutter. She'd been trying to get him to notice her, and the charity dinner was going to be her big chance to make an impression. But her father dragged her halfway across the country three weeks before the event.

Who was she kidding, though? Her father probably wouldn't have approved of Oliver. Just like he hadn't approved of the last three boys who'd shown interest in her. None were deemed "suitable for a husband." No one was ever good enough for him. Even her girlfriends. He didn't like that they'd gotten her involved in the women's suffrage movement. He was too old-fashioned to understand why it was important to her.

All she's ever wanted was to marry for love. To look at her husband the way Amy March looked at Laurie. But alas, she couldn't compare her life to characters on a page. And she needed to find a way to make the best of it. After-all, she knew very little about Harold Declan McAllister. The third. Maybe he's a dashing gentleman who's been unlucky in finding love and he's ready to sweep her off her feet. That was the hope. But she also feared his only reason for agreeing to the arrangement was for the money he'd be inheriting.

She'd find out soon enough. They were to meet her betrothed tomorrow.

Lifting her chin, the glare of the setting sun caught her eye and she looked up. A brilliant range of colors from yellow to orange and red hung just above the mountains. And for the first time she noticed them. Really noticed them. She'd been so consumed with *why* she was here that she hadn't really paid attention to *here* at all.

She found it difficult to look away; the beauty of the Rockies was breathtaking.

A cool breeze swept by Tillie, bringing with it a sweet floral fragrance from the mounds of yellow flowers in the pot beside her. She inhaled the sweet smell once more, then made the bold decision to go back inside. Not for the company and ambience, but for the first hot meal in nearly a week.

Chapter Four

____

Friday, 11:00 a.m.

The lunch bell rang, calling the men in from the field. Haying season had begun at Triple Peak Ranch and today they were working on turning what had been cut the day before. Hot, tired, and famished, Jacob jabbed his pitchfork into the ground and joined Nathaniel and Sebastian, heading toward the main house.

The three stopped at the well pump to clean up on their way in, as it was a rule in Yetta's kitchen if you wanted to eat.

"Where'd you go off to for so long yesterday?" Sebastian asked Jacob as they waited for their turn at the pump.

"Yeah," Nathaniel chimed in, handing the bar of soap to Jacob. "I saw you leaving—looked like you were all spiffed up."

"Oh, uh, I ran into Mr. Salzman the other day and he asked if I could help him out with some stuff down at the hotel." Jacob lathered up his hands and handed the bar off, nonchalantly adding, "Muscle work kinda stuff."

When neither of the men said anything, Jacob worried they'd object. He tried to get ahead of it.

"I hope you don't mind. It's just a few odd jobs and he feeds me while I'm there," Jacob said. "I told him the Ranch always comes first."

After a beat, Nathaniel finally gave in. "Well, all right. I guess it's fine as long as he's not trying to hire you out from under us."

"No, sir. You're my family. I'm not going anywhere." Jacob smiled.

"Better not." Sebastian slapped Jacob on the shoulder before turning toward the house.

Nathaniel's wife, Yetta stood on the front porch as the men approached.

She greeted her husband first, checking the cleanliness of his hands, then smiling as she turned her cheek. Nathaniel leaned in and planted a kiss, then stepped inside.

Sebastian and Jacob held out their hands for a quick look as they passed. Sebastian chuckled every time. The men found it endearing. As a teacher, Yetta was set in her ways. And those ways didn't stop just because it was summer break.

Once in the kitchen, Nathaniel was quick to scoop his daughter from her highchair. "Are you being a good girl and eating your lunch for Grandma Clara?"

At two, Charlotte was enamored by her daddy. She giggled and jabbered, as he bounced her on his hip.

"She's always a good eater," Clara replied. "Aren't you, baby girl? You love your beans and cornbread."

"She sure does! As PawPaw used to say, I don't know where the lil' p'nut puts it all," Yetta joked, using her best John Simpson impression.

Clara and John weren't family by blood, but they'd been with the Price family since Nathaniel was a small boy.

It had been said that Clara had practically raised Nathaniel and his brothers. And John, or "Simpson" as they called him before Charlotte came along, had been an integral part of the Price family business back in Texas. But that was before. Before Nathaniel's fallout with his father, and the subsequent termination that drove John and Clara to Nathaniel's door. As far as Nathaniel was concerned the Simpsons would be the only grandparents his children would know. And since the older couple had never had children of their own, they welcomed the responsibility with open arms. Sadly, they lost PawPaw about six months ago when his heart finally gave out.

Nathaniel kissed Charlotte on the forehead and placed her back in her seat.

Sitting across the table, Jacob flashed Charlotte a big smile and covered his eyes with his hands. After the count of three, he pulled his hands away, stuck out his tongue and crossed his eyes.

Charlotte squealed in delight.

"Is Uncle Jacob being silly, Charlotte?" Yetta asked as she placed a plate of bread on the table. Sebastian tried to reach in behind and steal a piece, but she swatted his hand. "Not until everyone is seated."

"Is my husband misbehaving again?" Ava asked as she entered the kitchen with a bit of a waddle.

Sebastian's wide eyes flashed to his wife. His smile full of guilt.

"There you are." He crossed the kitchen and embraced her from behind. "How's momma doing today?" he asked as his hand caressed her growing belly.

"Good," Ava answered, putting her own hands to her belly and closing her eyes. She swayed in his arms. "The baby is quiet now, but she was kicking up a storm this morning."

There was a time when Jacob was blind to the displays of affection between the couples. But now, at twenty-one, Jacob longed for a bit more in life. He longed for a woman —and a house—of his own.

He wasn't looking to leave Triple Peak Ranch. He loved his job—and being a part of Triple Peak family even more. They were all he had. He was seventeen when Nathaniel Price took a chance on him, giving him a job and a place to lay his head. And for that he'd be ever grateful. Before he found Nathaniel—or rather, Nathaniel found him—he'd bounced from town to town looking for work, or at the very least, food and shelter. He'd been on his own since the age of thirteen. Not even a horse to his name.

But sleeping on a straw bed in the barn didn't have the same appeal as it did when he was a kid. It's not that he hadn't had offers to stay in one of the three houses on the ranch, he has. But he relished his privacy and independence.

Jacob vaguely heard the conversation around him as he let his mind wander.

He imagined his arms around the curves of a particular woman

"That means you're having a boy."

"Have you come up with a boy name yet?"

"Not yet. We have a couple in mind."

"I vote for John."

A whisper in his ear, pulled him from his thoughts. "I know that look."

Jacob eyed Yetta, leaning over his shoulder. "What look?"

"Eyes gazing off. Smile on your face." With a grin, she hesitated. Then whispered, "You're thinking about a girl. You met someone, didn't you?"

"Maybe." Although it didn't matter because she was

betrothed to another. Besides, someone like Mathilda Coventry would never be interested in someone like himself. She was rich and fancy, and quite frankly seemed like a headache.

But then why couldn't he stop thinking about her?

———

It was mid-afternoon. Lunch service was over, and the dining room quiet and empty, save for a bit of noise coming from the kitchen as they prepared for dinner.

Tillie pressed her shaking hands together and buried them in her lap, hiding them under the table. With each minute Mr. McAllister was late, her hope rose that he wouldn't show at all.

Sitting to her right, her mother refolded her cloth napkin for the fourth time and pressed it flat with her hands. "Are you sure we got the right day?"

To Tillie's left, sat her father. He checked his pocket watch. "It's only been five minutes. I'm sure he's a busy man and these things are to be expected."

"I would think that *this sort* of meeting would be important enough to be on time," her mother groaned.

"What do you want me to do about it?" her father huffed. "He'll get here, when he gets here."

"The tea is getting cold."

"We can get more tea," he replied through gritted teeth.

Pursing her lips, Tillie squeezed her eyes shut. She felt trapped, sitting between her parents as they bickered. Wishing she could disappear, she did the next best thing and blocked them out.

She pictured herself standing on the stoop outside their home in the city. She imagined the street beyond their gate, busy with carriage traffic. She could hear it now: the clip-clop of the horses' hooves, the rattling of the harnesses, and the rumble of the wheels on the cobblestone street.

A hand landed on Tillie's arm, whisking her back to the present.

"He's here," her mother said with a hint of urgency in her voice.

Feeling faint, Tillie dropped her chin and sucked in a cleansing breath before looking toward the door.

Most of the boys in her social circle were in their early twenties, and she'd found that the majority of them were still going through a growth spurt. They hadn't quite filled out yet. But that wasn't the case with Mr. McAllister. At twenty-five, he was tall and stood with presence, puffing his noticeably broad chest under his vest and overcoat. She couldn't deny he was a good-looking man. He had striking, jet-black hair that was finely combed straight back, leaving no part. And with his dark eyes and dark, well-shaven muttonchops framing his face, the masculinity in his chiseled jawline were on full display.

When their eyes finally met, Tillie was disappointed. She was hoping for sparks.

Her father stood as the man approached. "Mr. McAllister, it's a pleasure to finally meet you in person. Your father has told me so much about you."

"Splendid," the man replied with a dry tone and piercing eyes, looking completely dumfounded.

Her father extended his hand. "I'm Theodore Coventry."

"Please, call me Declan," he said as they shook hands.

"Alright. Declan, it is." Her father smiled and glanced toward her mother. "I'd like you to meet my wife, Dorothy," he said, as she stood and raised her right hand gracefully.

"It's lovely to meet you," she said.

Mr. McAllister gently held her fingers and kissed the top of her hand. Then, he lifted his eyes to meet hers and replied, "You, as well." He certainly was debonaire.

But Tillie wondered if anyone else thought he seemed shifty, or that up close he looked markedly older than twenty-five.

Tillie's father put his hand on her back, and she rose to her feet, forcing a smile.

"And this … is my daughter, Mathilda," he said with a proud smile and a hint of grandeur as if she were the prize Mr. McAllister had come for.

But the man did not receive her in the way her father had intended. It was evident in the way his eyes roamed the length of her body. Tillie began to feel like a horse at auction. She was both offended and mortified.

Tillie's mouth drew a grim line.

She clasped her hands in front of herself and gave a curt nod. "Mr. McAllister." She addressed him formally. Coldly.

For a split second, a crease appeared between his brows and Tillie wondered if that was a sign of curiosity or hostility.

"Miss Coventry," he replied in return. His tone didn't seem one of curiosity.

Tillie's father gestured. "Please, have a seat."

As everyone took their seats, Tillie's father shot her a quick look of warning. This was not the first time she'd seen that look. Nor would it be the last.

Tillie's mother reached for the teapot sitting in the middle of the table. "Would you like some tea, Mr. McAllister?"

"No," he answered holding up a hand, practically

waving it away as if it was somehow offensive. "Never drink the stuff. Thank you all the same."

"Oh, sure, uh," her mother stuttered, keeping her hand on the pot. She passed an apprehensive look toward her husband.

After a beat of awkward silence, Tillie slid her cup and saucer toward her mother. "I would love some tea, mother." Her defiance—though small—gave her a bit of a thrill.

Her mother's mouth twitched into a smile. Deep down they were a lot alike, Tillie and her mother.

"How about you, Teddy dear?" her mother asked as she filled Tillie's cup. "Would you like some tea?"

"I think I'll pass today, thank you," he answered. Then addressed the other man, "Would you like something else? I can call into the kitchen."

"I got all I need right here." Mr. McAllister patted a hand to his breast pocket. The sound it made was strange, tinny and hollow.

After another uncomfortable moment of silence, her father attempted to make conversation.

"I don't know if you remember, but we actually met once," he said, nodding. "Yeah, eleven or twelve years ago —you were about fourteen—your parents hosted a dinner for a..." he hummed as he gazed away, snapping his fingers. "Gosh, what was his name ... the large fellow who was running for mayor?" Tillie could tell by the look on Mr. McAllister's face that he either didn't remember or that he didn't care. But apparently her father didn't pick up on that. "He was a one of your father's old partners. Do you know who I'm talking about?"

"I don't know," the man said simply, with a shake of his head. "I don't really recall much of my childhood so..."

his words evaporated into the air and the conversation died once again.

Now it was her mother's turn to try.

"Colorado is beautiful. How long have you lived in these parts?"

"Oh, uh just over two years."

"What made you leave New York?" her mother asked.

"Just wanted a little adventure before I was tied down with a job and family." Mr. McAllister pulled a silver flask from the breast pocket of his overcoat, unscrewed the top and took a swig. After returning the flask to its secret compartment, he settled back in his chair. "My father wasn't happy with my decision to leave. Do you know what his last words to me were?"

Tillie's father shook his head. "No."

One side of the man's nose wrinkled as he curled his lip. He leaned forward in his chair and tapped the table with his pointer finger. "My father's last words to me were 'I give it a year. Two tops. You won't last out there on your own.'" The man laughed. But it wasn't a happy laughter. This laugh, though short, bordered on disturbed. "Can you believe my own father had so little faith in me?"

"Well, I guess you showed him," Tillie's father replied with smile and a boost to the other man's ego. "You seem like you're doing just fine."

"Apparently not good enough because a couple of months ago, I get a letter from him that says … if I marry before my twenty-sixth birthday, he'd gift my inheritance in one lump sum upon receipt of proof—a marriage license. However," he said, holding up a finger. "Failure to do so would result in my disinheritance and upon my father's death, all monies would be equally divided amongst my sister and the Lower East Side Foundling Hospital in New York." He guffawed and went on. "I told my father it would take me longer than that to find a suitable woman in Colorado—there ain't many single ladies around here."

Tillie had a bad feeling about this match up.

Mr. McAllister waved a hand. "I'm sorry, I shouldn't be unloading my troubles on you all."

"No worries," Mr. Coventry said. He passed a glance toward Tillie, and then back to their guest. "Listen, that's just the way of life, son. Family don't always agree, and sometimes we have to do things we don't want to for the good of the family."

Tillie rolled her eyes. Her father couldn't have been more obvious.

"You must really like it here then," Mrs. Coventry said trying to rescue the conversation once again.

"Colorado?" He shrugged. "It's all right. I like the weather and the opportunities here."

That seemed to peak her father's interest. "What kind of opportunities?"

"All sorts of opportunities." He smirked. "You're only limited by your imagination."

"Aah," her father hummed as he stroked his chin. He had a look of curiosity and wonderment in his eye. "I like that. You're only limited by your imagination," he repeated.

What was happening? Had this stranger somehow put a spell on her parents? Why was her father so entranced by that ambiguous answer?

Tillie unclenched her jaw. Leaning forward, she straightened her back and placed one hand over the other on the table.

"So, tell us, Mr. McAllister … what opportunities has *your imagination* imparted you?"

There was that look again—that crease between his brows.

Mr. McAllister's eyes shifted toward her father; the corners of his mouth curled into a smile. He hitched his thumb. "This one's a little spitfire, isn't she?"

"That she is." Her father huffed a laugh through pressed lips and shot her another look of warning. Turning back to Mr. McAllister, he changed the subject. "I assume your father shared the details of our conversations—and arrangements—along to you?"

"Uh, what details might you be referring to?" the man asked with narrowed eyes and a slow shake of his head.

"About talking to the reverend to reserve Tuesday for the ceremony."

"Oh, *those* details. Yeah, yeah, we're all set."

"Excellent," her father replied with a smile.

If Tillie was a gambling kind of woman, she'd bet everything that Declan McAllister did not in fact talk to the reverend. She couldn't figure out what it was about the man, but she didn't trust him. Now she just had to get her parents to see him the way she did.

That wouldn't be easy.

Suddenly Tillie realized the conversation was going on without her.

"…and that reminds me, how many people will you be inviting? I need to let the kitchen know," her mother said raising her cup and taking a sip.

"People?" Mr. McAllister repeated. "Uh, I hadn't planned on inviting anyone. I thought this was going to be a small, intimate ceremony."

"My wife doesn't do small." Tillie's father snickered.

Mr. McAllister made a wry face. "Well, I don't have anyone I'd like to invite."

"Oh…" Looking perplexed, her mother's mouth hung open. Finally, she snapped out of it, waving her hand and feigning another smile. "That's okay. We've invited some of the guests who are staying here at the hotel, so it'll still be fun," she said passing a glance to her daughter.

Tillie felt as uncomfortable as her mother looked. And still her mother tried.

"You know, our Tillie was quite popular in the New York social scene," her mother said proudly, resting a hand on her daughter's arm. "So I'm sure she'll be eager to make friends and get to know the community."

The look on Mr. McAllister's face was somewhere between a grimace and a scowl. "Yes, well, I don't think there will be time enough in the day for that sort of thing —what, with all the chores to be done at home. I mean, between the cooking and cleaning, the laundry … the garden needs a lot of work, and it might be nice to get some chickens … and maybe some goats."

Her mother's face blanched with chagrin. "Oh, well of course, tending to the chores comes first. I just meant … it would be nice for her to have a little support as she learns the ways in such a new environment."

Mr. McAllister eyed Tillie again, one corner of his mouth curling. "I think she'll be fine. I bet she's tougher than she looks. Aren't you, Miss Coventry?"

Tillie knew he was challenging her. And she wasn't the type to back down. Look weak.

Her mouth stretched into a tight-lipped smile in attempt to hold back the devil on her tongue. Although, he was waiting for an answer. "I'm plenty tough. Thank you, Mr. McAllister."

The tension in the room was palpable.

Her betrothed licked his lips and leaned forward. "You don't like me much, do you?"

His bluntness surprised Tillie.

But it shocked her parents. In unison, they inhaled sharply.

"What? No!" her mother argued.

"Oh, I'm sure that isn't the case." Her father laughed awkwardly. "She's just a little reserved until you get to know her. Isn't that right, Mathilda? Tell him," he ordered his daughter.

Mr. McAllister threw a hand in the air. "It's okay," he interjected with a smile. Although he seemed to be addressing her parents, he held her stare. "I like a challenge."

Chapter Five

Friday, 2:55 p.m.

Jacob stood in front of the Grand Hotel, tucking his clean white shirt in again. He wasn't sure if he was more nervous about his second day working for Mr. Salzman or his third chance to make a good impression with Mathilda Coventry.

He took a deep breath and patted his horse's neck. "Wish me luck, Buddy," he said before turning toward the front entrance.

As he approached, the door opened and out stepped a man with thick black hair; it even creeped down both sides of his face. Jacob recognized the man from the Good Luck Saloon. He quickly lowered his chin and passed by, hoping the man wouldn't recognize him.

"Hey!" The man's voice made Jacob flinch.

Is he talking to me?

Continuing toward the door, Jacob glanced over his shoulder.

"We hit a snag," the man said, approaching another

man that Jacob hadn't noticed, but recognized just the same.

"And what would that be?" another man said, pushing away from the post he'd been leaning on.

Jacob quickly averted his eyes, lest he be seen.

"She didn't come alone."

Jacob was so focused on listening to the men's conversation, he nearly bumped into Alvin.

"Everything all right?" the bellhop asked, holding the door open.

"Oh, yeah, sorry," Jacob answered, glancing back one last time. "Hey, do you know why that man was here?"

"He was visiting one of our guests."

Phew! That was a relief. For a moment, he thought maybe the man was here looking for him.

Straight ahead, the door to the dining room opened and out walked Mr. Coventry. His wife and daughter followed close behind, arms locked together at the elbows.

"I'd like to speak with Mr. Salzman," Mr. Coventry said. "Is he available?"

"He's in his office," Alvin was quick to answer. He moved toward the door behind the front desk. "I'll let him know you're waiting to speak with him, sir."

"Thank you." Mr. Coventry then turned to Jacob. "Can one of you boys go with my wife up to our room and help her with one of the trunks? Darn thing won't open."

"I can go up and take a look," Jacob answered. He tried not to look too eager. But he couldn't believe his luck, walking in and seeing *her* straight away. His palms began to sweat.

"Thank you, son."

Jacob let his eyes pass over Tillie but was careful not to stare. "After you, ladies." He waited, then he followed them up the stairs.

Tillie leaned closer to her mother. "Do you think father is angry with me?"

"I really don't know."

Tillie glanced over her shoulder. Jacob quickly dropped his gaze to the steps in front of him, pretending not to listen.

"Honestly, mother, I really was trying." She groaned. "But I don't have a good feeling about this arrangement. Can't you talk to father?"

Mrs. Coventry sighed. "I've tried. You know I have. I don't know what else to say to him."

As they approached the first of their two rooms, the woman dropped her daughter's arm and stepped ahead, directing Jacob to the second—the room at the end of the hall. Tillie stood back to let him pass and even though she tried to hide it, he saw her wipe away a tear.

"It's that one over there," Mrs. Coventry said, standing in the open door, pointing toward the far corner. "It seems to have gotten banged up in our travels."

Jacob crossed the room and began inspecting the large wooden trunk standing on end.

"It's a wardrobe, supposed to be upright like that when you open it," Mrs. Coventry added.

Tillie plunked down in the settee. "I told you I needed a new one, mother. That one is probably older than I am."

Jacob ran his hand along the opening, feeling the metal straps for damage or imperfections. When he found the problem, he pulled his knife from his pocket and flicked it open.

"This one is fine. I'm sure he'll get it open in no time," her mother replied as he eased the sturdy blade between two pieces of metal and pried.

"So, what are you, anyway," Tillie began, "a waiter or a bellhop?"

Just as Jacob realized she was addressing him, the trunk popped open.

"See, I told you he'd get it," her mother proclaimed cheerfully. Then, with pause, she said, "I'm sorry, what was your name?"

"It's Jacob, ma'am," he answered with a smile, tucking his knife away.

"Well, thank you, Jacob. Once again, you've been very helpful." She tried to hand him another coin, but Jacob declined with a slight wave of the hand and a dip of his chin. He felt funny taking money in front of Miss Coventry. He had this need to look proud.

"It's my pleasure, ma'am."

He turned toward the door and Mrs. Coventry followed. "Might we be able to call on you, specifically, when we are in need of extra help, Jacob?"

Standing at the threshold, he met the woman's gaze. He felt a warm rush of appreciation creep up his neck. "I'd be happy to help—whatever your needs."

Her hands came together as if to clap. "Wonderful."

"Well, alrighty then," he said with a smile and a nod. "You ladies have a nice afternoon."

Jacob's gaze moved from the woman in front of him to the young lady on the settee. Their eyes met and with his new understanding, he realized the pain behind hers.

Holding her gaze, he slowly smiled and nodded again. "Miss."

He closed the door behind him.

TILLIE STARED at the back of the door.

A strange feeling fluttered in her chest. Her cheeks warmed, and her lips curled ever so slightly.

"Did you hear me?" The sound of her mother's voice yanked her back to reality.

Tillie released a quiet breath and wiped the smile from her face, cursing herself for being dazzled by those sparkly blue eyes again.

"I'm sorry, mother, what did you say?" With her sensibilities restored, Tillie rose to her feet and approached the small table where her mother had placed her fancy metal stationary box.

"I said, come help me write up some wedding invitations."

"What ever for?"

"Your future," her mother replied. "We'll go into town and hand out invitations to business owners, the banker, the doctor … whoever we can think of. It'll be the perfect way for you to meet people in the town."

"As long as it doesn't turn into a spectacle. Especially if —" Tillie hesitated to finish.

"Especially if, what?" her mother's tone was low and terse.

Tillie's brow raised with optimism. "If the wedding gets called off." She shrugged. "I mean, that would be a little embarrassing in front of all those people we don't know."

"The wedding is not going to be cancelled."

"Did you not see the way he looked at me when we first met? There was no attraction there, mother!"

"You'll grow to love each other," her mother said calmly. "He can give you a good life. You just need to give it time."

"How do you know he'll give me a good life? We know nothing about him," Tillie cried.

"He's a McAllister, Mathilda. They're old money. Status," her mother replied, composure waning.

"What good is his family name and status in Colorado? I doubt anyone here cares and I didn't get the impression he was real keen on moving back to New York anytime soon." Turning her back on her mother, Tillie rubbed her temples as the pressure in her head built. After a beat, she spun back. "And just because his family has money doesn't mean he is a good man. I'm telling you … I don't have a good feeling about him. I mean, you saw how he was."

"How was he?" Her mother scowled.

Tillie sighed. "Didn't his story about his father seem a little rehearsed to you?"

Her mother pulled back as if Tillie had offended her. "No, he seemed completely sincere to me. He may have been a little prickly but you sure weren't making it easy for him."

"Ugh," Tillie groaned, rolling her eyes and spinning away from her mother. "I think I would be better off with Jacob the bellhop-waiter at least he shows more interest in me."

"What's this, now?" her father asked, glowering as he stepped into the room.

Tillie sucked in a breath.

"Nothing, dear," her mother answered crossing the room to greet her husband. "How was your meeting with Mr. Salzman?"

"It was fine." He flicked a glance to Tillie, then back to his wife. "It doesn't sound like nothing. What's going on?"

Tillie's mother stood close in front of him, pressing her hand to his chest. "Really, dear. She was just trying to make a point."

"And what point would that be?" he asked. When his wife didn't answer quick enough, he looked to his daughter.

"Mathilda? Has something happened with an employee of this hotel?"

Tillie got to her feet.

"No, father," she answered, wide-eyed.

He turned his stare to his wife.

"No, Teddy. The boy hasn't made advances toward her in any way."

Her father pursed his lips and breathed heavy through his nose.

"I didn't mean anything by it. I was merely suggesting that Mr. McAllister didn't seem the slightest bit attracted to me. He looked at me as if … as if I were a piece of meat, or an inconvenience to be dealt with."

"Maybe if you had just sat there and smiled, but noooo. You had to go and open your mouth—"

"Theodore!" her mother huffed.

"Oh Dorothy," he groaned. "You know what I'm talking about. It was like she was going out of her way to be rude."

Frustration overcame Tillie.

"I'm going for a walk," she announced.

Slamming the door behind her, Tillie rushed down the stairs to the lobby and headed straight for the exit.

"Afternoon, Miss," the bellhop said, opening the door for her.

Tillie crossed the threshold and stopped, looking both ways.

"Can I help you find something?" the bellhop asked.

Finally, she acknowledged him.

"A quiet place to disappear," Tillie answered curtly.

His head cocked. "Is everything alright, Miss?"

Tillie felt tears prickling to the surface. When you come from a rich family everyone expects your life is perfect. So, no one had ever asked her such a question before. Taking a deep breath, Tillie blinked the tears away and shook her head.

"Is there something I could do to help?" he asked.

"I really just need some time to myself … away from my parents."

The bellhop cast a quick look back, into the lobby of the hotel. Then to her, he whispered, "Would you like me to take care of them for you?"

"Could you do that?" she asked.

"Sure." He grinned. He hitched his chin to the left. "There's a spot around back where the kitchen help hang out sometimes, you should be safe back there. And if your parents ask … I haven't seen ya," he said with a wink.

Chapter Six

Friday, 4:00 p.m.

Jacob grabbed another potato from the heap beside him. He wiped the sweat from his brow and groaned to himself. He'd already been peeling for close to an hour. How was there still so much more to do? This was the part of kitchen duty he did not like. Quite frankly, he'd rather be back on the ranch mucking stalls.

The door from the kitchen, leading outside, stood open, letting in a late afternoon breeze. It certainly helped the overall temperature as they worked, but from where Jacob sat, in an out of the way corner, he wasn't able to reap its full reward.

He finished the next potato and stood. "Hey, Jeremiah, I need to step out for a minute and get a drink of water."

Jeremiah gave a nod and Jacob stepped outside.

He turned to the water barrel which sat to the left of the door, picked up the ladle and chugged.

Wiping his mouth with his sleeve, Jacob turned.

"Oh, hello," he said in surprise, "I didn't see you over there."

Mathilda Coventry sat on a roughhewn log bench with her back to the wall of a neighboring outbuilding. The look she gave him seemed a combination between bashful and guilty. Had he intruded?

"I'm sorry, I'll leave you to your privacy." He started for the door then stopped and turned. His eyes roamed over the drab area around them—to the pockets of mud dotting the hardpacked dirt where dirty dish water had been dumped. Compared to the front of the Grand Hotel, the back was simple and lackluster. His brow pinched. "Wouldn't you be more comfortable sitting out in the front, Miss Coventry?"

Tillie pressed and unpressed her lips. "I'm perfectly comfortable here," she answered, patting the rough surface of the bench gingerly with her hand.

Jacob grinned. He didn't believe her. But who was he to argue.

"Okay. Have it your way." He shook his head and turned back toward the door.

"It's just—" she began, getting his attention again. His gaze met hers and she continued, "I needed to get away from my parents for a while."

He turned fully toward her this time and slowly closed the space between them. He wanted to ask about her intended marriage but thought it too bold. Especially since the topic seemed to upset her. Captivated by her beauty and elegance, he caught himself staring. His mind reeled, he needed to say something.

"You asked earlier, if I was a waiter or a bellhop," he blurted. She nodded with interest. "Well, the truth is … I'm neither."

Tillie's brow dipped. "Pardon?"

Jacob squatted and pulled a tall blade of grass from the edge of the dirt path. "It's just that … I recently found myself in a bind and Mr. Salzman helped me out." Resting on his heels, he plucked the wheat-colored seeds from the bushy top one by one and let the wind take them. "So, to pay him back, I'm helpin' out around here in the afternoons, after my other job—where I'm a ranch hand."

"A ranch hand," she echoed. "You mean like at a ranch with cows?"

Jacob grinned again. "Sort of. What we have is longhorn cattle."

"Is that a type of cow?"

"Uh, well," Jacob hesitated. He'd never had to explain such things before. "It's more like a *cow* is a type of cattle. It's what we call the females. The males are bulls—unless they're castrated, then we call 'em steer."

"Oh." Her eyes narrowed as if she were taking it all in. Filing away the information. "And what's low horn mean?"

"Low horn?" Jacob repeated. He thought back to their conversation, wondering what she was referring to. Then it clicked. "Ooh, longhorn."

He was surprised at how interested Tillie seemed.

"That's the breed. Just like with dogs, there are many different breeds. The longhorn is mostly raised for its meat. They have these great big horns" —he spread his arms as wide as he could— "that can reach up to like eight or nine feet from tip to tip. So, they look very different from the average dairy cow you've probably seen."

Tillie shrugged bashfully and confessed. "I've never seen a cow before … well, not in person anyway."

At the blushing of her cheeks, Jacob said, "That's okay. I'm sure there are lots of things in New York that I haven't seen before."

A soft smile lit up Tillie's face.

It was the first time Jacob had seen her smile. His lips curled in response.

"Do you miss it?" he asked. "New York, I mean?"

"Yes."

"I'm sorry you're so unhappy here—"

"These potatoes aren't going to peel themselves!" The voice from behind brought their conversation to an abrupt end.

Jacob stood and looked over his shoulder, to Jeremiah standing in the doorway.

"I'll be right there." The man disappeared inside, and Jacob turned back to Tillie. "Well, you heard him, those potatoes aren't going to peel themselves," he said with a lopsided grin.

Tillie's smile widened, she let out a snicker and stood, clasping her hands in front of her. "I'm sorry to have kept you. I do hope I haven't gotten you into trouble."

"Nah, it's fine," Jacob waved it off, backing toward the door. "Besides, I quite enjoyed the break."

"I did, as well," she replied.

At the threshold, Jacob paused. He wanted to stay and talk with her just a little longer. Make her smile again. But not only did he have to get back to work, he had to remind himself that—like it or not—she was engaged to be married. And further contact with this woman would only end in heartache. He had to think of her as one of the top shelf dolls at the mercantile. He could look, but he couldn't touch.

"Have a lovely evening, Miss Coventry," he said, placing a hand to his heart.

———

TILLIE MADE her way around the building and up the steps

to the front door. She hadn't realized she was smiling until the bellhop pointed it out.

"Looks like you're feeling better."

"Yes, I suppose I am." She stepped inside but stayed near the door, eyes scanning the guests milling about in the grand lobby. "Any sign of my parents?"

The bellhop shook his head. "Not that I've seen."

"Good." Tillie sighed with relief; grateful they'd allowed her some freedom.

Ever since the wedding announcement a month ago, she'd hardly spent a moment out of their sight. At least it felt that way. She was sure it was because they were worried she'd run off like her friend Lenore Jameson had. The difference between Tillie and her friend was that Lenore was in love with a different man and *they* ran off together. With no money and no prospects, Tillie knew she wouldn't get very far on her own.

THE MOMENT TILLIE walked into her room, the door between the two opened.

"She's back, Teddy," her mother announced as she rushed toward her daughter. "You gave us such a scare. Where have you been?"

"I just went for a little walk," Tillie answered casually. "I ended up finding a quiet little spot to sit and enjoy some fresh air."

Her mother groaned like she wasn't having it. "Your father was worried you weren't going to come back."

"Where would I go?" Tillie sighed. "I didn't think I was even gone for very long."

"It's been over an hour." Her mother took her in her arms and whispered in Tillie's ear. "He is so angry."

Heavy footfalls announced her father's presence. Tillie

and her mother parted to find him standing in the doorway between. The look on his face made Tillie shrink and turn her gaze to the floor. He was about to release a torrent on her.

She waited, shaking.

A moment later the close of a door could be heard from the other room. Tillie lifted her head to find her father was gone. She should have felt relieved, but she didn't.

Standing frozen in the middle of the room, Tillie's mouth hung open.

Her mother turned to walk away.

"I'm sorry," Tillie said. Her mother didn't respond. She continued to the table where the invitations were laid out and took her seat. Tillie didn't like the silence. "I said I was going for a walk. I had no idea it would upset you and father so." Nothing. "Mother, you have to believe me. I wasn't trying to make things worse, or, or … runaway. I just needed to clear my head."

Tillie's mother picked up her pen and dipped it in the ink. "We're just disappointed with your behavior today. Your father thinks very highly of Harold McAllister and he had such high hopes for this marriage."

Out of all the arguments they'd had on this particular topic, what her mother had just said hit the hardest. Tillie felt it deep in her gut, like a bullet wound. Crippling her. But instead of blood, she oozed shame.

Without another word, Tillie took a seat at the table. She grabbed a pen and a blank note, glanced at a finished invitation her mother had done, and began to write.

Save for the scratching sound of pen on paper, the room was disturbingly silent.

Tillie finished the first, set it aside, and grabbed another blank note.

"You've always had such beautiful handwriting," her mother said.

"Thank you."

"I wasn't in love with your father when we got married, you know."

The statement came out of nowhere. An innocent confession. Almost as if the words have been bottled up for the entire twenty-two years they'd been married and she finally had the courage to let them out.

Tillie's eyes lifted to meet her mother's. They were glazed in fear, as if she has committed the ultimate sin and God would strike her where she sits.

"He didn't know, and I didn't want to break his heart." A tear trickled down her mother's cheek. "He had been pursuing me for so long … I'm sorry," she whispered.

Tillie's brow dipped. "What are you sorry for?"

"I just didn't want you to think of me as a hypocrite for forcing you to marry out of convenience over love. I'll admit at first it was hard but I'm happy with how my life turned out and I'm proud of our little family—"

Scooting her chair back, Tillie rushed to her mother's side and wrapped her arms around her, shoulders and all. "I am too," she cried, resting her cheek on top of her mother's head. "I am too."

Chapter Seven

Saturday, 9:05 a.m.

The next morning as Tillie and her parents finished their breakfast, a clerk from the front desk approached their table.

"Excuse me, Mr. Coventry?"

Her father looked up at the man. "Yes."

"There's someone in the lobby who would like to speak with you," the clerk said. "Says his name is Declan McAllister."

"Oh, uhh..." Clearly dumbfounded, her father brought his gaze down to Tillie and her mother. "Wonder what this is about?"

Neither woman could offer a guess.

Her father wiped his mouth with his cloth napkin, set it beside his plate, and faced the clerk again.

"Would you mind showing Mr. McAllister to our table?"

The clerk gave a nod, turned, and left the dining room.

A minute later, the clerk returned with Mr. McAllister.

"Here you are, sir," he said, pulling out the empty chair opposite Tillie. "Can I get you something to drink? A menu perhaps?"

"No, thank you. I won't be staying long." The clerk left and Declan took his seat. "I apologize for interrupting your breakfast."

"It's quite alright," her father replied. "Are you sure you wouldn't like a coffee or something to eat?"

"I guess a coffee does sound nice." Declan's gaze moved around the table. "If you're sure you don't mind."

"Of course, we don't mind," Tillie's mother said with a welcoming smile, while her father waved a waiter over and ordered another coffee.

The corners of Declan's mouth curled. Then his eyes moved from the older woman to Tillie.

"Good morning," he said with a smile.

Tillie was taken aback. He seemed so different today.

She smiled. "Good morning."

"What brings you by on this fine morning?" Tillie's father said, breaking Declan's gaze.

"Oh, right." Declan pulled an envelope from a pocket inside his overcoat. "It was obvious there was some tension between us yesterday and I thought maybe a marriage contract would show respect and put everyone's mind at ease."

He slid the envelope toward Tillie's father.

"A contract, you say," her father said, reaching for the envelope.

"Yes, I realized I might've given the wrong impression at our first meeting when I went on about the tension between me and my father." Declan paused, leaning back as the waiter placed a cup in front of him and filled it with steaming hot coffee. "Thank you," he said to the waiter before continuing. "So anyway, I wanted to show that I'm committed and that you haven't come all this way for nothing."

"How very noble of you. We have come a long way"—her father passed a glance toward Tillie—"and we *sure* wouldn't want anyone to back out now."

"I've already signed it." Declan pulled a fountain pen from the same pocket and placed it on the table between them. "I still have time to get it to the judge before he takes off to go fishing for the afternoon."

Tillie tried to hide her consternation. But the complete change in his disposition was telling her something wasn't right. Although, she worried any argument from her may only make her father sign faster.

She held her breath, her chest fluttering as she watched her father unfold the papers. There were three pages. Beside a couple of spots where specifics, like names and dates, were handwritten, the rest looked like long blocks of typed legal jargon.

Declan sipped his coffee as her father began looking over the contract and reading aloud.

"Contract of marriage agreement between Harold Declan McAllister III and Mathilda Coventry, who agree to be married on or before the twenty-third of blah blah blah…" He skipped further down the page, mumbling some words to himself and reading others aloud. "…shall live together at the husband's homestead beginning day of marriage and take on daily chores … to provide husband with child if heir is required…" He continued skimming the page. All the while, Tillie silently prayed he wouldn't sign it now. As he turned to the next page, he commented, "This all looks pretty straightforward."

Tillie couldn't stay silent any longer.

"Daddy," she whispered sweetly, placing her hand on his arm. His eyes left the page and met hers. "There is a lot to read there. I really don't think it's too much to ask for Mr. McAllister to give you a little more time to look it over and get it back to him." Her gaze landed on the other man, daring him to fight her on this. *What are you up to, Declan McAllister?*

But her father didn't give him a chance.

"I don't want to insult the man after he's gone to all the trouble to show good faith," her father replied. He flipped to the third page and uncapped the pen. "Where do I sign?"

"At the bottom—beneath my signature."

As the tip of the fountain pen glided over the paper, her father commented, "I want what's best for my daughter and I think you have the ability to give her a good life."

"I'll do my best, sir." Declan gathered the papers into the envelope and tucked them back into his coat pocket.

Tillie's eyes fell shut.

It was done.

She knew there was no getting out of it now. Which also meant moving forward with the plan to deliver the wedding invitations.

IT WAS close to eleven by the time Tillie and her mother left the hotel. Other than the short walk from the train station on the day they arrived, they'd yet to see much of the town. The town that would officially be Tillie's new home in three short days.

She wasn't sure what to make of Colorado Springs. At first glance she was overcome with culture shock. It was so very different from anyplace she had ever been. Although her only travels till now had been limited to cities along the east coast. The kind of cities that were built mostly of stone and brick, both their buildings and their streets. Cities with sidewalks and streetlights and bustled with people who needed to be somewhere.

The streets of Colorado Springs may have been busy, but no one seemed in a rush. In front of the Barber Shop, two men sat in wooden chairs. Feet resting on the railing in front of them, their chairs rocked back on two legs. Neither spoke. They just sat there watching the world go by.

And everything was so brown. From the dirt and mud in the streets to the buildings made of wood. Even the clothing the people wore were seemed to blend into the background.

Tillie felt slightly out of place in her baby blue silk dress and her matching parasol.

The first few stops they made went well. Tillie's mother did most of the talking. The people of Colorado Springs seemed friendly and welcoming. Though strangely, very few seemed to know the man Tillie was about to marry. Back home in New York it could be expected, but in a small town like this…

Tillie didn't dare cast doubt on the man, though. Not yet anyway. Not after everything that happened yesterday.

"Millie's Kitchen," her mother said cheerfully, closing her parasol as they approached the next stop. "Why don't we sit a spell and have a bite to eat?"

The place was deep and narrow with a single aisle down the middle and four small tables on either side. While it lacked décor of any kind, the smell of fresh baked breads and stews made it feel homey. Along with the fact that six out of the eight tables were full. Millie was obviously quite popular.

As Tillie and her mother stood near the doorway, a woman about Tillie's age came toward them. She held a heaping plate of food in each hand and balanced a third on her forearm.

"Have a seat. I'll be with you shortly," she said as she delivered the plates to a table nearby.

The ladies took a seat at an empty table and looked up at the menu written on a chalkboard hanging from the wall:

~Today's Specials~
Oxtail Stew
Veal Pot-pie
Fried Trout with Boiled Potatoes and Succotash
Apple PieMince Pie
Tea or Coffee

A FEW MINUTES LATER, the young woman approached their table, taking a deep breath and wiping her brow with the back of her hand. "What can I getcha?"

"We'd like to try the oxtail stew, please."

"Good choice. Nobody does oxtail like my mother." She smiled. "You new to these parts? Haven't seen ya 'round before."

"We are," Tillie's mother answered with delight. "Although, I'll be heading back to New York in a couple weeks. But my daughter Tillie here, will be staying."

"Oh, really?" She brightened, facing Tillie. "Nice to meet ya, Tillie. I'm Maggie. What brought you all the way out here?"

Tillie pressed her lips together and cleared her throat. "I'm, uh, getting married." The words felt strange coming out of her mouth. But she had to start getting used to it.

Her mother quickly chimed in. "His name is Declan McAllister. Do you know him?"

Eyes narrowed, Maggie turned at the waist and shouted over her shoulder. "Hey Jim, you know the name McAllister?"

Three men sitting at a table catty-corner, stopped talking and looked up.

"Yeah," one of the men—assumingly Jim—answered. Others in the small restaurant quieted to hushed tones, seeming more interested in this conversation. "He's the one who bought Grausgrubers place. Why? He done something?"

"Naw, just asking," Maggie waved him a nevermind and turned back. She hitched her chin. "That's the Sheriff. I figured he could help. I know who you're talking 'bout now. Don't see much of him in town—seems the type who likes to keep to his business."

A voice from the kitchen called out, "Order up."

"Gotta get that," Maggie said spinning on her heel. "Back in a jif."

"I guess that explains why he doesn't want to invite anybody," Tillie's mother said.

Tillie grimaced and said nothing. Even though this only brought up more questions than answers.

A few minutes later, an older woman brought their lunch out.

"Are you Millie?" Mrs. Coventry asked as the woman set the plates down.

The woman wiped her hands on her apron. "I am."

"We just arrived in town a few days ago for my daughter's wedding and we thought it might be nice to invite some of the fine people of Colorado Springs." Her mother handed Millie the invitation and continued, "We're having a little gathering at the Grand Hotel. We'd love it if you and Maggie could come."

"Well, that's right kind of you." Millie glanced at the invitation. "Tuesday at two … I think that might be doable seeing as it's between the lunch and dinner rush. I'll speak to Maggie and see what she thinks."

"Great. We hope to see you."

Millie grinned and tucked the invitation into a skirt pocket, beneath her soiled apron. "I gotta be getting' back to the kitchen."

Tillie took a bite of the stew. "Mmm, this is really good."

When they were nearly finished with their lunch, Maggie came by again. "Did you ladies want any pie?"

"I don't think I could eat another thing," Tillie moaned. "That was so good, but I'm absolutely stuffed."

"I don't have any room for pie either." Her mother laughed. "What do we owe you?"

"Here ya go." Maggie placed a small piece of paper, face down on the table. "Mama told me about the invite. We'd love to come." As she gathered their dirty dishes, she bent slightly and whispered, "Mama was so touched to be invited. She don't get out much."

Maggie flashed a big smile. Then, with her hands full, she headed back to the kitchen.

Leaving the money for their bill on the table, the ladies stood and adjusted their skirts before heading toward the door.

"Bye, Tillie. See ya again soon," Maggie called out behind them.

Tillie waved in return and stepped outside, pulling the door closed. With a smile stretching her face, she commented, "I like Maggie. She seems really nice."

Tillie's view of Colorado Springs had definitely improved.

After checking out the Post Office, the millinery, and the Daily Gazette, Tillie and her mother came to the Mercantile.

The bell above the door rang to announce their entrance. Though small, the shop seemed to carry a little bit of everything, from baking essentials to hatchets, to toys and fabric.

The ladies approached the clerk at the counter.

"Good afternoon, I'm Dorothy Coventry and this is my daughter Mathilda," her mother said.

"Nice t' meet ya. I'm George O'Brien," the man spoke with a bit of an Irish accent, "proprietor of this here establishment. What can I do ya for?"

"We just arrived in town a few days ago for my daughter's wedding," she said, gesturing toward her daughter standing beside her. At this point, tired of the same rigmarole, Tillie wandered away from the counter and browsed the shop.

Running her hands over the bolts of fabric, Tillie realized why the townspeople wore such dreary colors; they had very little selection available to them.

A woman approached the opposite side of the table. "If yer lookin' for sometin' special, we can order from de catalogue." By the sound of her thick accent, Tillie assumed this was Mrs. O'Brien.

"I'm just looking. Thank you," she replied.

"Did I hear yer marryin' Mr. McAllister?"

Suspicion crept into Tillie's mind. "Yes."

"I didn't realize he was still in town. Could ya do me a favor? His special-order tea came in and he hasn't been in t'pick it up—"

"Tea?" Tillie repeated. "What kind of tea?"

"Dat English tea he likes. It's been sittin' here well over a month. Would ya mind takin' it t'him?"

"Why, of course. I can do that."

"Splendid." She smiled and disappeared through a doorway in the back.

Tillie passed a glance toward her mother, happily chatting with Mr. O'Brien—though she couldn't hear a word. She was too busy, going over the growing list of questions in her mind.

Why would Mr. McAllister special order tea if he never drinks the stuff?

And why has he let his special order sit at the mercantile for so long?

Something just didn't add up.

"Here ya go," the woman said grabbing Tillie's attention as she stared off in thought.

Tillie took the small package. "Can I ask you something—Mrs. O'Brien—is it?"

"Yep, dat's me, Shannon O'Brien," she answered. "What else did ya need?"

"How well do you know Mr. McAllister?"

"Oh, uh, not dat well—keeps t'himself mostly," she said. "Used t'come in every few weeks for essentials, but not so much lately."

Tillie's brow furrowed. "Hmm, any idea why?"

"Oh, I couldn't say for sure." Mrs. O'Brien's mouth quirked in the corner, she looked away thoughtfully.

Tillie could tell the woman knew more.

"Please." She glanced back to be sure her mother wasn't listening. Then stared into the woman's eyes and lowered her voice. "You can tell me anything…"

Mrs. O'Brien hemmed and hawed. Finally, she spoke with caution, "I tink he's a very nice man, but he may have gotten himself int' a bit of trouble."

"What kind of trouble?"

Mrs. O'Brien stretched her neck, scanning the room. Then she stepped closer and turned, standing shoulder to shoulder with Tillie. Their backs to the front of the store.

"Money trouble," the woman answered. "Word has it, Mr. McAllister likes t'frequent de Good Luck Saloon. Owes some people a lot of money."

"Does he owe you money?"

"Two dollars and forty-two cents."

Tillie reached into her reticule, pulled out her change purse, and counted out two dollars and forty-two cents. She handed the money to Mrs. O'Brien.

"Tank you," the woman smiled. "I'm glad he decided t'stay and I look forward t'getting' more acquainted wit ya."

"What do you mean … that he decided to stay?"

"Oh, well, I tought he was tryin' t'find a way t'pay off his debt and move back east."

Out of everything Tillie had just heard, this surprised her the most.

But it gave her hope.

With the money they would receive after they wed, he could pay off his debt. Maybe *then* they could move back to New York.

"One more thing … uh, this is rather embarrassing," Tillie said. "I haven't been to his house yet. Could you tell me how to get there?"

Chapter Eight

____

Saturday 2:00 p.m.

With the town behind them, it seemed they could see for
miles.

"Why would you agree to deliver a package to his
house?" her mother griped. "I don't feel comfortable
showing up unannounced."

"I'm curious, mother." Tillie marched ahead. "I want
to see what the house looks like. After all, it is going to be
mine soon too."

"What's gotten into you? Why are you in such a
hurry?" her mother complained. "Are you sure we're even
going the right way?"

"Yes, mother." Tillie rolled her eyes, then stopped and
turned, waiting for her mother to catch up. "Mrs. O'Brien
said it's not that far out of town. She said to head west over
the railroad tracks and turn left just *before* the creek. If we
go over the Monument Creek bridge, then we've gone too
far, and we'd be heading into Colorado City territory.
From there, it's only about a hundred yards."

"Why couldn't we have had the hotel coach take us?" With her parasol in one hand, her mother lifted her skirts, stepping lightly around a rut in the road. "I'm not going to be happy if I ruin these shoes, Mathilda."

Tillie cocked her head. "You don't have to come with me."

Stopping in her tracks, her mother stood straight and tall, drawing her head back. Tillie had clearly offended her. She tried to cushion the blow.

"I just mean that I'll be fine on my own if you don't want to come." Her mother's eyes flashed to the ground and back. "Truly, mother. Why don't you go back to the hotel and rest?"

"I don't know..." Her mother relaxed a bit, entertaining the idea. "Are you sure? How do we know it's safe?" she asked, eyes scanning the horizon.

Tillie scanned too. There was nothing to see, other than rolling hills of prairie grasses swaying in the breeze.

She retraced her steps, going to her mother's side, and placing a hand on her mother's shoulder. "I really don't think we have anything to worry about. I've managed the streets of New York on my own, I think I can do this."

"But why do you insist on going now?" Her mother continued to argue. "We can come back later in the coach."

She blinked slowly and exhaled. "Because I had a heart to heart with Mrs. O'Brien and I'm wondering if I've misjudged Mr. McAllister."

Her mother's eyes brightened, her hand went to her chest. "Really?" she said with a gasp. "That's wonderful news. What ever did she say to change your mind?"

"That's not important right now." Tillie grinned, narrowing her eyes. "Mr. McAllister said he likes a challenge ... well, so do I."

And the challenge here for Tillie was to help Declan pay off his debts and agree to move back to New York.

After a beat, her mother grimaced. "You promise you'll be all right?" Tillie nodded. "And you'll be back before dinner?"

"I promise."

Tillie's mother kissed her on the cheek and turned back toward town.

Alone, Tillie marched on, her parasol the only reprieve from the hot sun.

Finally, a rickety bridge came into view.

She thought the water must be rushing because she could hear it from a good distance away. Or at least she thought that's what the sound was. Though the closer she listened the less it sounded like the rush of water.

CH-CH-CH.

She wasn't quite sure what was making the sound … until she was almost on top of it.

Rattlesnake!

Body coiled, head and neck poised to strike, the snake sat at the edge of the grass—just four or five feet from her.

Tillie froze. Afraid to take another step. Her only weapon, a baby-blue ruffled parasol.

She lowered the tip of her parasol slowly toward the ground, holding it between her and the snake as if she could hide behind it or bat it away if it were to move closer.

BANG!

The ear-splitting gunshot caught Tillie by surprise. As did the bullet hitting the snake, sending it flying back and leaving a trail of blood in its wake.

Shaking, Tillie blinked several times. As if somehow, this would erase what had just happened from her memory. Then slowly, she turned her head.

The stranger holstered his gun and jumped down from his horse.

Shock and fear kept her feet planted and her eyes on the man as he walked toward her.

He had hair the color of copper. It was thick and full, peeking from the bottom of his hat and spreading across most of his face; it even covered his shirt collar.

The pounding of her heart echoed in her ears. She shrank away.

Was he going to hurt her?

To her relief, the stranger walked past her and picked up his kill.

"This'll make good eatin' tonight," he said.

Tillie swallowed hard, nodding her head.

"What's a gal like you doin' out here all by yer lone-some?" he asked as he strung the snake from the back of the saddle.

"I'm on my way to see my fiancé. His place is just up there," she answered, pointing off to the left. She wanted to make it known that not only was she spoken for, but that he was close by.

The man's gaze followed the direction of her finger, then landed back on her. "Oh yeah?" He glared, pausing a moment. "You wouldn't happen to be the Coventry girl, would ya?"

"I am." While she was still shaking in her shoes, she kept her chin up and her voice steady. She fumbled with the small box as she closed her parasol and hooked the end over her arm.

"Well, I happen to be headed that way." His smile revealed a mouth full of half-rotten teeth. "The name's Rusty. Come on, I'll give you a ride." He gestured her over, then clasped his fingers together and straightened his arms, offering her a step up.

Wide-eyed, she drew her head back. "I'm not getting up there." Her hand absently glided over her silk skirt.

"Aaaah." He nodded as if he'd realized her reservations.

Then before she could object, he grabbed her waist with both hands, lifted her up, and plopped her down on top of the horse. She opened her mouth, ready to demand he get her down, but the man interrupted.

"Hold these," he said, handing her the reins.

She took them. "Sir, I must insist you get me down from here this instant." But he already had one foot in the stirrup and the other sweeping over the horse's back.

With both of Tillie's legs hanging over one side, the man settled in behind, taking the reins, and placing one arm on either side of her. He clicked his tongue and tapped the horse with his heels. And off they went, this strange man practically cradling her.

Tillie held her breath. Not only was she horrified by her current predicament, but she also couldn't stand the smell. The man surely had not bathed in quite some time.

They turned off the main road and followed the creek for a while. Finally, Tillie saw a small, white, two-story house up ahead. To the side of the house was a small barn and a corral with three horses. She never thought she'd be so anxious to see Declan McAllister again, but she'd give anything to get off this horse and away from this man.

From a distance the small house seemed almost charming but as they got closer, it started to lose some of its charm. The picket fence in the front was in desperate need of repair; surely in its current state it wouldn't contain a chicken, much less a goat. And it too, looked to have been white at one time.

The horse slowed to a stop and the man jumped down.

"Come on out and look what I brung ya," Rusty

shouted as he led the horse to a nearby hitching post. He wrapped the reins loosely and moved to help Tillie down. The way she was situated, her back was to the house. He reached up and grabbed her by the waist. Her hands went to his shoulders to steady herself as he lowered her to the ground.

Boot heels on the front porch could be heard just before the voice, "What took you so long? You didn't run into any trouble, did you? I swear to God if you done something to mess this up, I'll—"

Tillie stepped out from behind the horse.

McAllister looked at her and then back to the other man, his mouth agape. "What in tarnation…"

Rusty walked through the rickety gate. "I saved her from a rattler, down near Monument Bridge," he said. Then answered the next question before McAllister could ask it. "She was on her way here to see you."

Timidly, Tillie approached, holding out the package she'd been solicited to deliver. "This is from the mercantile, Mrs. O'Brien said it had been sitting there quite some time and she thought you might…" she let the words fall away as he held her stare and took the package. She noticed the familiar crease between his brow and looked away uncomfortably. "Well, uh, I'm sorry. It looks like I've come at a bad time. I'll just be going." She turned and took a step.

Declan exhaled gruffly. "Wait."

Tillie turned back.

He forced a smile. "I'm sorry, I just … you, uh, caught me off-guard is all. Please, stay."

"What about the—"

Declan cut the other man off. "You go on ahead without me. Tell them something came up and I won't be able to make it this afternoon."

Tillie smiled. She liked the feeling that he seemed to be

making her a priority. She also liked that he was sending the other man away.

"Did you get the contract delivered all right?" she asked.

"Uh, yeah," he answered. "Caught the judge just in time—would you like to come inside?" he gestured toward the door.

She nodded.

He seemed nervous.

The door opened into the kitchen and he stepped in first.

"If I knew you were coming today, I would've cleaned up a little," he said putting the package down before scrambling to clear a bunch of papers from the table. He scooped everything up in one armful and stuffed them into a nearby jelly cupboard.

Curious.

As he continued to tidy, Tillie let her gaze roam about the kitchen which stretched off to the left. Then she wandered through the open doorway on the right, it went to the sitting room. The furniture was sparse and what he did have seemed out of place. Far too nice for the surroundings. It was like he wanted the fancy things he was used to from home, but he hadn't really committed to staying. Still, it wouldn't have hurt for him to dust once in a while.

He must have read her mind because he said, "I think maybe it needs a woman's touch."

Tillie turned to face him. She smiled and nodded.

Rubbing the back of his neck, his eyes wandered the small kitchen. "Gosh, I don't have anything to offer you."

She moved back into the kitchen and gestured to the package on the table.

"You have tea." She watched for his reaction,

wondering if he remembered telling them he never touches the stuff.

"Oh, right. I can put on some water if you'd like."

Tillie attempted polite nonchalance. "Only if you want some too." This felt like a game to her—a game to see who would break first. But it seemed he'd come prepared to win.

"I recently stopped drinking tea because it was bothering my stomach," Declan tossed back smoothly, without missing a beat.

But the game wasn't over yet.

Tillie lowered her eyes, running her hand over the scrollwork on the back of the chair in front of her. "Mrs. O'Brien was telling me that you were considering heading back to New York."

That caught his attention.

"I think Mrs. O'Brien is a gossip and she doesn't know what she's talking about." The crease was back.

"I don't think she meant any harm," Tillie eased. She regretted bringing up the other woman's name. She liked Shannon O'Brien and hadn't meant to put her on the spot like that.

Feeling her heart beating faster, Tillie realized she needed to change her tactics. She was never going to get the answers she was looking for if he kept bristling like that.

"There is another reason I wanted to come out," Tillie simpered.

"And what's that?" He placed his hands on his hips.

"I'd like to invite you to join us for dinner tonight."

"Oh?" He seemed surprised.

"I realize that we were *both* feeling pressured by our families and it wasn't fair of me to behave the way I did."

Tillie lowered, then batted her eyes. "So, I was hoping maybe we could try starting over."

"That sounds like a fine idea. Why don't we head into town right now," Declan said, taking a step toward the door.

Tillie felt like he was in a rush to get her out of his house.

Her eyes fell on the jelly cupboard again. She didn't want to leave until she saw what he'd so anxiously hidden away.

She slyly hung her parasol from the back of the chair in front of her, then followed Declan to the door.

"After you."

She nodded, holding her breath as she crossed the threshold. She'd never felt so cunning in her life.

Declan closed the door, turned, and offered his arm.

Tillie smiled. "How very gentlemanly," she replied with a smile, wrapping her hand around the crook of his elbow.

They walked together, arm in arm down the front path and through the gate. Then Tillie stopped short, putting on a show as she looked down at her arms. "Oh dash, I must've put my parasol down."

"I'll get it for you."

Tillie patted his arm with her free hand. "Aren't you sweet? It's okay, I'll get it while you ready the wagon." His lips formed a straight line, not quite a smile. She could tell he wanted to argue, but she didn't give him a chance. Releasing his arm, she turned on her heel. "I won't be but a minute."

Once inside, Tillie hurried to the kitchen window and peeked out toward the barn. When she saw that he was pushing the large doors open, she made a beeline to the jelly cupboard and pulled out the stack of papers.

They were mostly hand-written letters from his father,

she noted as she quickly flipped through. But then a different letter caught her eye, dated just a few weeks after the last one from his father.

DEAR FATHER,

After giving your latest letter much thought, I have decided to move back east. While my time in Colorado has been one of adventure and self-exploration, I think it would be nice to be near family again. In fact, I would like to take that job you mentioned, if the offer still stands.

I have a few things to tie up here but plan to board a train by weeks end. I will send a telegram with my expected arrival at that time.

See you again soon.
Respectfully,
Your son,
H. Declan McAllister

TILLIE'S MOUTH HUNG OPEN.

Why didn't he send this letter?

Why didn't he leave Colorado?

She craned her neck, looking out the window again. When she didn't see Declan, she worried he was coming. So, she shoved the papers back into the cabinet.

A page, folded in triplicate, fell to the floor.

Hands shaking, Tillie looked toward the door and quickly bent to pick up the page. She threw it on top of the rest, but as she went to close the cupboard door, the title, marked in bold, fancy print, caught her eye: *Quit Claim Deed.*

Giving pause, she picked up the paper. Her entire body shook, scared she'd get caught snooping.

But she had to know if he was hiding anything.

Declan's name was written at the top of the page, along with a date coinciding with the letter to his father. And directly underneath was the word *to* and then another name. *Reed Larson.*

Had Declan signed his property over to this other man?

Tillie felt sick over what she was about to do. But she had to get out of the house before he got suspicious.

Stuffing the document down the front of her top, she closed the cabinet, grabbed her parasol, and hurried to the door.

Whipping it open, she stopped dead in her tracks.

Declan was coming up the walk, his eyes fell on her.

She stepped out and pulled the door closed behind her. "Sorry I took so long. After all the sun today, I was parched," she said, putting her hand to her chest.

"All right." The crease between his brow said it was less than all right.

Something in her gut clenched and twisted. She had to keep up the show.

"You weren't worried about me, were you?" she replied playfully.

He forced a smile. "The wagon is ready. Shall we?" he gestured with a sweep of his arm.

A few minutes later Tillie and Declan were on their way to town. To Tillie, it felt like the stolen document burned against her skin. Every moment they were together, she worried he would *know.*

Chapter Nine

Saturday, 3:15 p.m.

The 3:15 train arrived a few minutes early. Passengers were already off-loading when Jacob pulled up in the hotel coach.

The middle-aged couple saw *The Grand Hotel* scrolled in gold lettering on the side and approached.

"You must be the Carlsons," Jacob said.

"That would be us," the husband replied.

Jacob tossed the suitcases onto the back and helped the guests up to the passenger bench behind the driver's seat.

Hopping into the front, Jacob grabbed the reins and gave them a slight flick.

"How was your trip?" he asked over his shoulder as the horses began moving.

"Long," the wife answered.

"But fairly smooth and uneventful," the husband added.

"Good to hear," Jacob replied. "Is this your first trip to the Springs?"

"It is and it's the furthest west we've ever been," the man said.

"Where are you from?"

"Pennsylvania."

Chin to shoulder, Jacob tipped his hat and smiled. "Well, welcome to Colorado."

As THE COACH drew closer to the hotel, Jacob noticed a wagon parked in front. A man stood on the ground, his back to Jacob, helping a woman down. They were quite far away, but he would recognize Tillie anywhere. Although, he wasn't sure who the man was, other than to say that it definitely was *not* her father.

With her feet on the ground, the man's hand went to the small of her back. So, Jacob assumed it was her fiancé.

A bit of jealousy turned his stomach.

Jacob pulled back on the reins, slowing his team and averting his eyes.

While he was curious about the man Tillie would be marrying, he also couldn't bear to see them together. Especially with his hand on her.

By the time he pulled the wagon to a stop, the couple had gone inside. Still, he took his time helping unload the guests and their bags.

Thankfully, Alvin took over from there.

And to avoid any chance of running into Tillie and her betrothed, he circled around to the back of the hotel and entered through the kitchen.

"How many do you need for tonight, Jeremiah?" he asked, grabbing a small knife, and flinging a fifty-pound sack over his shoulder.

Jeremiah looked up from what he was doing, his brow arching high and lips slightly parting.

Jacob's brow dipped. "What?"

"No one's ever offered to peel the potatoes before." He laughed. Then, shaking his thoughts, he added, "Uh, about half should do."

Jacob settled into the chair in the out of the way corner, straddling the metal bucket designated for the peelings. Then, with the sack on one side and a massive pot on the other, he grabbed the first potato. Resting his elbows on his knees, Jacob hunched over the bucket, and got started. While this particular job wasn't his favorite, it did have two things going for it. First, that he didn't have to be on his feet, and second … it required no thinking. And being that it was his third day working both jobs, he was plum tired.

He'd been at it a while—already dumped the bucket once—when his mind wandered to Tillie. He pictured her from the day before, sitting on the bench behind the hotel. He'd replayed their conversation over so many times in his head already. But here he was again. He couldn't help it— it was so perfect.

She was so perfect.

Which was surprising because after their first interaction she had seemed completely unapproachable. Miserable, in fact.

But she was so easy to talk to. *And her smile…*

Jacob's cheeks warmed and he realized he was smiling.

I must look like an idiot … smiling and peeling potatoes, he chuckled to himself.

But the way that she looked at him…

He felt something. And he would swear she did too.

Then a pretentious thought entered his mind, *has* he *been able to make her smile?*

Jacob knew he had no right to think with such arrogance, but he was aware of how unhappy she was with the pairing.

That's when his mind went to the other man's hand on her—touching her in such an intimate way.

Jacob dropped the potato in his hand. "Ow, dangit!"

Blood oozed from a two-inch slice along the heel of his palm.

He put the knife down and pressed his thumb over the wound to slow the bleeding as he made his way out the back of the kitchen.

Immediately his eyes went to the right—to the log bench. But as expected, it was empty.

Turning to the water barrel, left of the door, Jacob picked up the ladle and rinsed the blood from his hands. Then he grabbed the handkerchief from his pocket and quickly wrapped the wound.

His eyes drifted to the bench again and he smiled. He thought it funny that the crude bench behind the beautiful Grand Hotel would forever hold a special place in his heart.

"How bad are you hurt?"

Jacob spun around to see Jeremiah standing in the doorway.

"I saw the blood on the floor," Jeremiah replied. "How bad is it?"

Jacob lifted his hand, lowering his eyes. Blood was already seeping through the cloth. "It's not that bad. Won't need stitches or anything."

Jeremiah waved him in. "Come on, let's wrap it a little better."

A few minutes later, Jeremiah had completely rewrapped Jacob's hand, using fresh clean bandages.

"There ya go," he said, finishing the knot. "You're off potato duty. I don't want bleeding in my kitchen."

"But—"

"Go," Jeremiah interjected with his arm extended, pointing toward the door.

Jacob left the kitchen and headed toward the front desk of the hotel, looking for Mr. Salzman for his next order of duty. Instead, he was intercepted by Alvin.

"Oh hey, are you available?" Alvin asked.

"Yes, what do you need?"

"A guest needs help up in room eighteen."

With that, Jacob turned and made his way up the stairs to the second floor. He hadn't paid attention to how the rooms were numbered before, so he wasn't sure which way to go. The door across from the stairwell was marked "Room Eight" and to the right of it was "Room Ten."

Jacob went down the hall to the right. All the even numbers were on the left. He continued down the line: twelve, fourteen, sixteen…

Jacob stopped as the realization hit.

Room eighteen was the last room on the left. The room belonging to Mathilda Coventry.

He took a deep breath, stepped forward, and knocked on the door.

———

TILLIE DIDN'T LIKE the way Declan had come in and taken over, questioning the boxes and trunks stacked in her room. And insisting that everything be moved out to give her more space.

"Really, this stuff isn't bothering me," she said. "We don't have to do this right now … before dinner."

"*We* won't be. That's why I asked the hotel to send someone up," Declan argued. "Besides, I'd rather get it done now and not have to worry about it after the ceremony."

"It's not like we would have to move everything that day. My parents will be staying here for a while."

"How long?"

"They haven't decided yet. Maybe a couple of weeks."

Tillie watched the expression on his face. He seemed bothered.

She looked toward the door adjoining the two rooms, silently wishing her parents would hurry. Her mother had been resting when they arrived, and her father had gone in to wake her.

Tillie and Declan had only been left alone five minutes. But that was all it took for him to stir up trouble.

Knock. Knock.

"There's the help now," Declan said as he crossed the room.

Tillie stood back, hoping it was anyone other than Jacob.

Declan pulled the door open and immediately started giving orders. "I want all the boxes and trunks brought down to my wagon and someone to watch over the things until we're finished with our dinner." Whoever Declan was talking to was not in Tillie's line of sight.

She held her breath, waiting for the person to speak or step inside, but it seemed they were taking forever to respond.

"Well," Declan prodded. "Get to it."

"Oh, yes of course. Sorry sir."

Tillie's eyes fell shut as she recognized the voice.

"All of them, sir?" Jacob asked as he stepped inside.

"I said all of them, didn't I?"

"No, not all of them." Tillie boldly stepped forward.

Jacob's eyes met hers and Tillie wished she could disappear.

"You shouldn't need more than a dress or two to get by," Declan replied.

Tillie's chest tightened. He made her needs sound so trivial. The more time she spent with this man, the harder he was to figure out. Take her luggage for instance, at first, he made it sound like he had her best interest in mind. Like, he would be helping her out by getting everything moved and giving her more space. But when she mentioned the luggage wasn't bothering her, he became more adamant. And now, he was downright disrespecting her.

Tillie turned from Declan to Jacob, curling her lips slightly and pretending she wasn't about to have a break-down. "If you could leave that trunk for me"—she pointed to the one nearest the modesty screen—"I would really appreciate it."

Jacob nodded. "Yes, Miss Coventry."

The pained look in Jacob's eyes matched the pain Tillie felt. He reached for one of the trunks first, grabbing the leather strap on the end and lifting.

"If anything turns up broken or missing, I'm holding you personally responsible," Declan said as Jacob dragged the trunk toward the door.

Tillie winced.

Jacob didn't respond. He didn't even pass a glance to Declan.

Before Jacob and the trunk crossed the threshold, the door to the adjoining room opened.

"Sorry for keeping you waiting. Dorothy is freshening up—" Confusion registered on her father's face. "What's going on? Where is he taking that?" he asked, looking between Tillie and Declan.

Tillie's mother stepped through the door and took in

the room. The same look of confusion spread across her face. "What's going on?"

"I told him to bring her things down to my wagon," Declan said. Tillie flashed a look toward her mother as he continued. "I wanted to get everything moved now, so we don't have to hassle with it all later."

"Oh, I guess that makes sense," her father answered, then gave a nod to his wife as if wondering if she agreed.

"I suppose that might be helpful," Tillie's mother replied with a shrug and a shake of her head. Placing her hand on her husband's arm, she said, "Maybe you should go help him. I don't know how he's going to get it down the stairs by himself."

As Tillie's father headed toward the door, she eyed Declan, arching her brow. Luckily, he took the hint and followed the other men.

"I'll probably need to direct them to my wagon, anyway," he grumbled.

With the men gone, Tillie reached down the front of her dress.

"What are you doing?" her mother croaked.

"I don't think Declan's being truthful with us," she answered, pulling the document free.

"What is that?" Her mother's eyes grew wide. She swiped the document from Tillie's hand. "Did you steal this from him?"

"No, I'm just borrowing it so I can get a better look. I'll put it back."

Tillie's mother examined the page, her jaw slacking. She looked up, with furrowed brow. "I don't understand."

"Me either. Why would he sign his property over to someone else?" Tillie reached for the document.

Her mother held it tight. Still staring at it. "But where did you get this?"

Tillie took a deep breath, pondering how much to tell her mother.

Finally, she started with what Mrs. O'Brien had told her—the reason Tillie had been suspicious that he was hiding something. And that the way he scurried to tuck the papers out of sight had only spurred her suspicions further. Tillie ended with the letter to his father—the letter that confirmed what Mrs. O'Brien had said about him planning to return to New York.

Tillie grimaced. "I told him that Mrs. O'Brien mentioned that she thought he was leaving town."

"What did he say to that?"

"He denied it and besmirched her name," Tillie answered.

"But it doesn't make any sense that he would still have this," her mother said, holding up the document again. She thought a minute. Her features softened. "Unless maybe he found a way out of his debt or a reason to stay and changed his mind?" Tillie saw the optimistic hope in her mother's eyes. She always tried to see the good in people.

"Then why not just come clean about it?"

Her mother sighed in dismay, then pivoted and crossed through the open adjoining door.

Tillie followed. "What are you doing?"

"They'll be back any moment, we have to hide this," she said as she bent and stuffed the document under the mattress. Her mother straightened, rested her hand on the bodice of her dress, and blew out a cleansing breath. "We speak nothing of this until we find out more information. Do you understand?"

Tillie nodded, meekly. "Yes ma'am."

Chapter Ten

Saturday, 4:00 p.m.

Jacob kept his head down while in the other man's presence.

What was his name again? He'd heard it the other night in the dining room.

Dean McAllister? No, Declan … Declan McAllister.

Although Jacob knew him as The Boss. And he worried that at any moment The Boss would recognize him. Sure, the man ended up getting his money, but Jacob still worried he'd find a way to drum up trouble.

Seeing Tillie with him made Jacob physically sick.

How could she marry someone like that?

Did she know that the man with whom she's betrothed was a low-down hustler and a cheat? Not to mention, employs two goons to do his dirty work for him.

After the trip down the stairs with the first trunk, Jacob enlisted Alvin's help, relieving Tillie's father and fiancé. The two couples retreated to the parents' room to chat, while Jacob and Alvin cleared the luggage from Tillie's room.

When they were done, Jacob knocked twice on the doorframe between the rooms. He stood in the open doorway. "Pardon me," he said. "I wanted to let you know that we're finished in here."

"Remember what I told you," McAllister said. "It's your hide if everything is not there and in pristine order."

"I'm sure everything will be just fine," Tillie said to her fiancé.

He brushed her off, raising his brow to Jacob, waiting for a response.

Jacob noticed Tillie shrink in her seat. He appreciated her trying to advocate for him, but frankly, he didn't want her getting between them. God forbid the man take his frustrations out on her.

Jacob pressed his lips together and gave a nod. "Of course."

Back downstairs, Jacob pulled all the coins he had from his pocket and offered them to Alvin. "This is yours if you can do me a favor."

"Really?" Alvin smiled. "What's the favor?"

"I need to leave to check on something and I need you to cover for me while I'm gone and also keep an eye on Miss Coventry's things," he said gesturing toward the wagon sitting out front.

"Um, I don't know." Alvin looked between Jacob, the wagon, and the clerk at the front desk.

"Please," Jacob begged. "I wouldn't ask if it wasn't an emergency."

"What if someone finds out you aren't here and that I

lied?" Alvin whispered, even though they were well away from everyone.

"No one will know." Jacob kept his voice low, matching Alvin's volume. "I'll be quick—back before the dinner service is even under way. I promise."

Alvin huffed. "Alright. But you better make it fast," he warned.

Jacob dropped the coins into Alvin's hand and headed out the door. He went straight to Mr. McAllister's wagon and took a few minutes to cover and secure everything. Not only for the sake of his own hide, but also so he could easily slip away.

———

The Coventrys still had a good forty-five minutes to entertain Mr. McAllister before they could head to the dining room for dinner.

"Why don't we take this downstairs to the lobby, where we'll be a little more comfortable?" her father suggested.

"That sounds like a fine idea," her mother replied.

"Agreed." Declan stood.

Tillie rose with the rest. "I'd like to take a few minutes to freshen up after my trek across the prairie," she said. "How about I meet you downstairs shortly?"

With that, the others left, and Tillie adjourned to her room.

Closing the door behind her, she leaned back against it and took a breath. She needed a few minutes alone with her thoughts.

Could mother be right, and Declan simply found a way out of his problem?

Am I making a big deal of nothing?

While she didn't like that he'd insisted on moving her

things, was he truly just trying to make things easier for her?

Then there was the way he treated Jacob. Why did that bother her so? She'd surely witnessed worse in New York.

Could it be I have feelings for…

Tillie shook her head, refusing to finish her thought. She pushed away from the door and stripped out of her dusty dress. After splashing some water on her face, she unpinned her hair and gave it a good brushing. Her light brown hair hung in waves below her shoulders. It felt good to let it hang loose, especially since she had washed it the day before. She decided to leave it down, pinning just the front back but leaving a few tendrils to frame her face.

Tillie went behind the modesty screen and pulled a pink flowered dress from a hanger. It was one of her favorites. She slipped it on, gave her cheeks a pinch, and headed out the door.

Midway down the stairs, she spotted her parents and Mr. McAllister across the lobby. It looked like her father and fiancé were deep in conversation. They seemed to get along well. Better than she did with the man, anyway.

The conversation came to an abrupt end when she approached, her father seeing her first. The men rose from their seats.

Her father smiled. "You look beautiful."

"Thank you, Daddy." Her eyes moved to her fiancé.

The corners of his mouth were almost curling up. And he almost had a sparkle in his eye.

Tillie blushed. She'd seen that kind of look many times before—even knew by the silence that her looks were pleasing.

"Ahem," Declan cleared his throat, shifting his eyes away. It seemed he didn't like getting caught admiring her.

While the men returned to their seats and continued

their conversation, Tillie's mother quietly commented, "Did you see that?" She smiled, leaning closer to her daughter. "He certainly seems attracted to you now."

Tillie snickered and waved her hand. "Stop. He'll hear you," she whispered, her cheeks growing warmer.

A short time later, Mr. Salzman and the gentleman from Chicago approached the two couples. Tillie was embarrassed about the way she'd spoken to the other man at dinner their first night here. She hoped to let him know it, in some way, without bringing too much attention.

"How's your visit been so far?" the hotel owner asked with an enormous smile.

Tillie's father stood, offering an equally large smile.

"Very well, thank you." The men shook hands and then her father gestured to Declan, who had also gotten to his feet. "This here is Declan McAllister, my daughter's fiancé," he said. "Declan, this is Edgar Salzman. The owner of this fine hotel. Edgar is another north easterner—hails from Boston if memory serves me."

"That is correct," Edgar replied before shoving his hand toward Declan. "Nice to meet you."

"You as well. Beautiful establishment you have here."

While the three of them were engaged in their introductions, Tillie met Mr. Hawthorn's gaze. Tilting her head slightly, she flashed him a timid smile and batted her eyes.

Lips pressed together, he smiled back and gave her a nod.

Mr. Salzman slapped a hand on Hawthorn's back, diverting his attention. "And this is Steven Hawthorn, my marketing man from Chicago."

Tillie and her mother sat quietly while the four men carried on. She watched how Declan interacted with the other men. He smiled and seemed quite personable.

Maybe he wasn't so bad?

———

ATOP HIS HORSE, Jacob rode at a full gallop. Never slowing until he crossed into Colorado City and had the Good Luck Saloon in his sight.

He figured the best time to go asking questions was when he knew exactly where his subject would be. And that was back at the Grand Hotel, having dinner with the Coventrys.

He tied his horse off and went inside.

There weren't any poker games going at the moment and a couple of men he did recognize, looked like they were well roostered up and not likely to be of any help.

Jacob approached the bar.

"What'll ya have?" the man asked as he wiped a rag over the countertop between them.

"Uh, I was just hoping you could tell me what you know about Declan McAllister," Jacob said.

The man's arm stopped moving, he held the rag in place.

"McAllister?" the man grunted. "I haven't seen him in here in probably a good month or two."

"No," Jacob argued, his brow pinching at the center. "He was here just a few days ago. So was I. We sat at that table over there"—he pointed—"playing poker."

The barkeep stared blankly at Jacob.

"You must know who I'm talking about?" Jacob continued, growing aggravated. "They call him The Boss, he comes in here with his two hired hands…"

At that, the man walked away, going to the other end of the bar and cleaning glasses.

Jacob moved down the bar. "You know who I'm talking about, don't you?" he asked quietly.

"You gonna order something, or not?" The barkeep kept his eyes on the room.

"Yeah, sure." Jacob reached into his pockets. He figured the man might be willing to talk if he spent some money in his establishment. But he'd forgotten that he'd given all his money to Alvin. "Dangit, I don't have any money on me."

"I don't want any trouble in here," the barkeep said under his breath before meeting Jacob's gaze. Arms spread, he rested his hands on the bar. One side of his mouth quirked into a condescending grin. "Well then, you have a nice evenin', sir," he said in a firm voice, heard around the room.

Jacob had clearly been dismissed.

Chapter Eleven

Saturday, 6:00 p.m.

Tillie was surprised how well dinner with Declan seemed to be going. She found herself finally relaxing and enjoying herself.

In fact, she didn't even tense when the marriage agreement was mentioned.

"Oh, that reminds me," her father said, directing his attention to Declan. "Were you able to get the marriage contract delivered in time?"

"I did," Declan answered. He raised a glass toward Tillie and smiled. "We're as good as married—"

A sudden crash of shattering glass broke through the din. The dining room quieted.

Tillie looked over her shoulder to see what all the fuss was about.

A waiter had dropped a stack of dirty plates and silverware. He was bent over the mess, collecting the pieces. It wasn't until he stood, that Tillie realized the waiter was Jacob.

Their eyes met and Tillie quickly looked away.

A moment later he was squatting beside her.

"Excuse me, Miss, there's a piece of glass under your chair." He reached in and pulled it out. As he got to his feet he whispered in her ear, "Meet me behind the hotel."

"You were saying?" Tillie said as she raised her glass and met Declan's gaze.

It took everything she had to keep her hand from shaking.

Declan stared deep into her eyes as if reading her thoughts.

She forced a smile. "Is something wrong?"

"Did he say something to you?"

Tillie lowered her glass. "Yes, he said there was some glass under my chair."

"Is there something going on with you and him?"

A cold chill ran down Tillie's chest and arms. She didn't like the intense tone of his accusation.

"Me and the waiter?" she guffawed. "Don't be ridiculous."

"Is he bothering you?" Her father's brow furrowed. He'd been cold toward Jacob since her comment the day before. The stupid comment that she never should've made.

Then Declan chimed in again. "I can tell something is going on because you were acting strange when he showed up at your door to take care of the baggage."

"Would everyone just stop! He's not bothering me and there's nothing going on between us," she said with agitation, addressing both men. Then she threw her napkin on the table and leveled her stare at Declan. "And quite frankly, I can't believe you'd accuse me of such a thing when the evening was going so well." She got up from her seat. "Now if you'll excuse me, I'm going to the loo to calm down. Or are you going to question *that* as well?"

Head held high, Tillie marched out of the dining room.

When she was sure the coast was clear, she headed out the front door.

"If anyone asks, you haven't seen me," she said as she passed Alvin.

Alvin winked. "You got it miss."

Before she disappeared around the side of the hotel, she checked again to be sure she wasn't being followed.

Tillie found Jacob behind the hotel, pacing and wringing his hands.

She was upset at him for the scene he caused and ready to let him have it, but then she noticed the bandage on his hand.

She gasped. "Did you cut yourself on the glass?"

He looked down at the bandage like he'd forgotten about it. "No, this happened earlier." He shrugged it off and blurted, "You can't marry him."

While Tillie was flattered by this boy's attention, she grew angry. Crossing her arms in front of her chest, she let him have it.

"I appreciate that you were nice to me when I needed someone to talk to and I apologize if I led you on in some way, but you have no right to be jealous. Or tell me what to do!"

"No, that's not—"

"Let me finish," she snapped, cutting him off. She waved a stiff finger toward the hotel. "I came to Colorado to marry that man and while things may have started off a little rough, I am dedicated to making it work—for the good of my family. So, you need to stay out of my business. You're making this harder for me. Things were finally starting to improve, but now he thinks there's something going on between me and you."

"But he's not—"

"Stop! I don't want to hear it." Tillie put her hand up, closing her eyes and turning away. Why was he fighting her on this? He knew from day one that she was betrothed. She hated to be so harsh, but it had to be done. "I'm marrying Declan McAllister on Tuesday and until then … I need you to keep your distance. Don't make me report you to the owner of the hotel," she said as she turned, fixing to make a quick exit.

"Tillie, wait, you have to listen to me!" Jacob grabbed her by the arm, spinning her back.

Tillie looked down at his hand. His touch stirred something in her—a desire she shouldn't be feeling. A desire she hadn't felt when Declan touched her.

A myriad of emotions collided in her chest, making it hard to breathe.

She couldn't allow Jacob so much control over her. She had to remember what was at stake, and channel the anger and resentment again.

Lifting her chin, Tillie leveled her stare. "How dare you address me so informally."

"I'm sorry." Jacob released her arm and took a step back. "It's just … he's not who you think he is."

"Oh really? Who is he, then?"

His lip curled with uncertainty. "*That*, I'm not sure of yet."

Tillie snickered, cocking her head. "Well then, until you have actual facts to share … leave me alone."

Tillie ran toward the front of the hotel, quickly ducking around the corner and pressing her back to the wall. She took several long breaths, willing herself not to cry.

It took all she had to remain strong in front of Jacob.

She didn't want him to know he was getting to her or that she'd already had her doubts regarding Declan McAllister. If only Jacob had tangible evidence of what it was Mr. McAllister was hiding...

But he didn't.

And the fact of the matter is, unless they had some kind of proof they'd been deceived in some way, Tillie was about to be Mrs. Declan McAllister.

For better or for worse.

A FEW MINUTES LATER, a headstrong Tillie returned to the table, a smile plastered on her face.

Declan hopped up and pulled out her chair.

"I apologize," she said as she settled into her seat. "I don't know what came over me."

"Maybe you got too much sun today," her mother suggested. "You do look a little flushed."

Her father waved a waiter over. "Can you get my daughter some more water, please?" Then to the table, he said, "I just read an article about altitude sickness. Maybe we should talk to a doctor?"

"No, I'm fine. Really," Tillie replied. "I'm sure it's just nerves."

Finally, Tillie's gaze landed on Declan. She couldn't read his expression.

She swallowed nervously, lifting her fork, and looking around the table. "I hope everyone wasn't waiting on my account," she said, taking a bite of her now-cold dinner.

Tillie's parents quietly went back to their meal.

Not Declan.

Though she tried to ignore it and enjoy her meal, she felt his eyes boring into her.

"So if you're not feeling sick, what took you so long?"

His words triggered a memory from earlier in the day. Declan had asked the exact same thing of the stinky redhaired man who'd saved her from the rattle snake.

She thought back to that moment just before he saw her. What else was it he'd said?

"You didn't run into any trouble, did you? I swear to God if you done something to mess this up, I'll—"

There was so much aggression in his voice.

Three questions came to Tillie's mind.

What were those two up to?

What was he about to say?

And ... *was Declan McAllister capable of violence?*

A shiver ran down Tillie's spine. The bad feeling was back.

And worse ... this man was actually starting to scare her.

"Are you sure you're all right, dear?" her mother asked, getting her attention again.

Tillie blinked a couple times. "Maybe I am a little tired."

———

No matter what Tillie said, Jacob wasn't about to let it go. He had to do something. Had to tell someone.

He knocked on the office door.

"Come in," Mr. Salzman said.

Jacob opened the door and stepped inside. "Sorry to bother you, sir."

Edgar Salzman sat behind his desk. He looked up from his work. "Hello there, son. Did you need something?"

"Uh, I've got kind of a problem," he said, cringing and shoving his hands in his pockets. "Well, uh, it's not really *my* problem but..."

"Spit it out, son. You're rambling."

"Sorry, I'm just not sure where to begin."

Mr. Salzman rose from his chair and circled to the front of the desk. Leaning against the edge, he crossed his ankles. "What is it, boy?"

Jacob took a deep breath. "You know the man Miss Coventry is here to marry?"

"Sure, I met him this evening." His brow dipped. "What about him?"

"I don't think he's who they think he is."

"And why is that?" Jacob heard the skepticism in the hotel owner's voice.

"Because I've met him before," Jacob said. "Only, I know him as the one they call The Boss."

"The Boss," Mr. Salzman repeated, eyes narrowing in thought. "You mean…"

"Yeah. He's the one who accused me of cheating and nearly had me killed. He is not a good man, sir. Miss Coventry can't marry him!"

Mr. Salzman sighed and rolled his eyes.

"Jacob," he said as he stood and went back behind his desk again. "If you're going to continue to work here until your debt is paid off, then you need to stay out of other people's business. Especially the guests."

"But sir—"

"Just because you and Declan McAllister had a dispute, you cannot go around tainting his reputation." Hands on his desk, Mr. Salzman leaned forward. "I get it, she's a beautiful young woman and maybe you're smitten. But you need to stay out of it."

"But that's just it—he's not Declan McAllister," Jacob replied.

Mr. Salzman straightened. "What do you mean *he's not* Declan McAllister?"

Jacob rubbed the back of his neck. "I wanted to find out more about him—to see what kind of man he really is —so I went back to the saloon and asked the barkeep about him." Jacob paused, cringing again.

As expected, Mr. Salzman didn't approve. His brow knitted and shoulders slumped. "You didn't?"

"I know it was a stupid thing to do," Jacob spat. "But listen, when I mentioned McAllister's name, the barkeep said he hadn't seen him in at least a month." The hotel owner's expression fell slack and Jacob went on. "I told him that couldn't be because I had played poker with the man just a few days before. And so, thinking the barkeep was confused, I mentioned that he goes by "The Boss" and travels with two hired hands. That's when the barkeep clammed up and asked me to leave."

The hotel owner shook his head. "You're going to get yourself killed." He blew out a breath and looked away. Rubbing his chin, he faced Jacob again. "You haven't said anything to the Coventrys about this have you?"

Jacob grimaced. "I tried to warn Mathilda. But she wouldn't listen."

Salzman groaned. "Please just stay away from that family and the fiancé. Don't make things worse. Tomorrow we can talk to Sheriff Walker and see what he has to say."

Jacob heard the man's pleas, but he couldn't make any promises.

Chapter Twelve

Saturday, 7:35 p.m.

Jacob stood in the hotel lobby, his mind a flurry of thoughts as he stared out a front window at the wagon loaded with Mathilda Coventry's belongings.

What was he to do?

How was he to prove Declan McAllister was an imposter?

Jacob was so focused on the problem at hand that he'd ignored the activity around him. Until a familiar voice caught his attention.

"Are you sure you can't stay for coffee and dessert?" Mr. Coventry asked.

"I wish I could, but I have to get home and unload the wagon before it gets too dark." The voices were getting close. With his back to them, Jacob listened.

"Ah, yes. I do hope you can manage everything by yourself."

"Yeah, I'll be fine."

Now they were upon him.

"Okay. I'll see you at church tomorrow, then."

The men said their goodbyes and parted ways. Jacob waited until The Boss was nearly at the door before making his presence known.

"Miss Coventry's things remain safe and secure, just as you asked." Jacob turned and stepped closer, hands folded behind his back.

The man stopped in his tracks, obviously caught off-guard.

But Jacob knew he had a part to play and by golly he was going to play it.

"Have a good evening, sir." He stuck his hand out, palm up, like he'd seen Alvin do, requesting a tip for his service.

The man scowled and reached into his pocket. Jacob had to force himself not to smile at the irony.

The coins dropped with a clink into Jacob's palm.

He curled his fingers around them and smiled. "Thank you, sir."

Without a single word, The Boss walked out the front door.

Jacob stuffed the money in his pocket, vowing to add it to the jar by his bed, along with the other tips he's made over the last few days. It would all go toward paying off the debt he owed to Mr. Salzman.

From the doorway, Jacob watched the man lope down the steps and approach the side of the wagon, stopping to check the tie on the canvas cover. He gave it a tug before moving on toward the front.

Then as the man lifted himself up to the driver's seat, Jacob made a rash decision.

With a quick look around to see if anyone was watching, Jacob rushed out the door and down the steps. Keeping his eye on The Boss as he pulled away, Jacob hurried to catch up—careful to stay directly behind the wagon so as not to be seen.

As Jacob closed in, he grabbed the back of the wagon with both hands and lifted himself up. The toes of his boots clung to a small ledge where the base and the rear board came together. He used one hand to flip the cover up, then rolled himself over the edge and into the back along with Miss Coventry's luggage.

Laying in the dark, beneath the cover, Jacob struggled to catch his breath. More than the short jaunt, it was his nerves that winded him.

What was he thinking?

And what the heck was he going to do if he got caught?

———

AFTER SEEING DECLAN OFF, Tillie's father returned to the table.

"Did you two decide what you want for dessert?" he asked as he took his seat.

"I think I'm going to get a slice of huckleberry pie," her mother answered.

"I'm going to skip dessert tonight," Tillie said, pushing her chair back and standing. "It's been a very long day, so if you don't mind, I'm going to go up to bed."

Her mother reached for Tillie's hand and looked up at her solemnly. "Sleep well, my dear."

"Good night. I hope you feel better in the morning," her father said as she left the table.

As Tillie weaved her way toward the door, she discreetly scanned the dining room for Jacob. She'd suddenly felt that she'd made a grave mistake pushing away the only person who was actively looking out for her.

With Jacob nowhere to be seen, she checked the hotel lobby.

"Can I help you with something, miss?" Alvin asked.

She stepped closer and whispered prudently, "Have you seen Jacob?"

"He's right over there," Alvin answered as he turned and pointed toward a window in the front. But the window was empty. "Oh, well, he was there just a minute ago. He was keeping an eye on the wagon with all your things."

Tillie's dinner turned in her stomach. She rushed out the front door, worried she'd find Declan and Jacob having it out in the street.

But to her relief, she spotted Declan driving away and Jacob nowhere in sight.

Once the wagon disappeared around the corner, Tillie went back inside.

"Would you like me to tell him that you were looking for him?" Alvin asked.

"No, that's quite all right," she said a little too hastily. Then smiled and gave a nod. "Thank you. Good night, Alvin."

"Good night, miss."

———

Peeking through a slit in the cover, Jacob could tell the wagon had turned and was heading west out of town. A few moments later, he recognized the familiar *thump-thump* of the wheels crossing the railroad tracks. And not long after that, the hollow echo as they crossed the Monument Creek Bridge.

It was when the wagon turned to the south, away from Colorado City, that Jacob began to keep track of landmarks along the way. They were heading into unfamiliar territory for him.

The task became much harder as darkness fell.

Finally, the wagon slowed.

"Whoooaaa," the man grunted, directing his two-horse team.

Jacob peeked out and saw light up ahead.

He quickly slid out of the back of the moving wagon, tumbling and rolling to a stop. Staying low, he crawled for cover behind the nearest outcropping.

A campfire lit a wide area in front of a rundown farmhouse. Two men sat on log benches around the fire, legs stretched out in front of them, a drink in one hand, and rolled tobacco in the other.

Jacob recognized the men.

While the hired hands focused on the arrival of The Boss, Jacob snuck closer, keeping to the shadows. He made his way around to the side of the house and hid between two stacks of wood. By the looks of it, the wood had been sitting there for several years, leading Jacob to believe the property had been deserted long ago, and these men were squatters.

Sitting on his haunches, Jacob peered through a gap between some logs.

"Whatcha got there?" the larger of the two men asked as The Boss hopped down from the wagon. The tip of his cigarette glowed orange as he took another long puff.

"Why don't you get up off your behind and come take a look," The Boss answered, flipping the cover back.

The hired hands stood and walked over to the rear of the wagon.

"Is this all from that high-falutin gal I met this afternoon?" the red-haired one asked.

"Yep."

"She sure did smell nice," the man said with a perverse smile. "I hope you plan on passin' her 'round when yer done with her." He cackled and nudged the larger man with his elbow.

The two broke out in laughter.

Every muscle in Jacob's body tensed. Fists shaking at his sides, he held himself back as the rage boiled to the surface. But he had to keep his wits about him. He was no match for three armed men, he wouldn't make it two feet before getting himself shot.

While The Boss worked to pry the lid off one of the wooden boxes marked fragile, the other two pulled down one of the trunks and threw it open. Jacob watched in disgust as their filthy hands rifled through Tillie's clothing.

The larger man pulled out a dress and held it up in front of himself. His voice rose to a higher octave. "Hello there handsome." He batted his eyes dramatically, put his hand up to his mouth, and blew a kiss to his partner. "What's your name?"

"Rusty," the red-haired man answered, playing along.

"Well, Rusty, what's a lady gotta do to get a dance around here?" he sang, still holding up the dress as he swayed and twirled.

Rusty chortled, waggling his red, bushy eyebrows and taking a step toward the other man.

"Put that away before you ruin it!" The Boss barked.

"What's it matter? She ain't gonna be needed it," the larger man replied.

"Until that inheritance comes, I have to keep up appearances. Besides, we can get money for all this stuff."

The other man grumbled and tossed the dress back into the trunk.

"That sure was smart gettin' them to sign that weddin' agreement," Rusty said. "I took it to the Postmaster and sent it like we did that last letter you wrote to the father. Also sent the telegram just like ya asked."

"Did the Postmaster seem suspicious?"

"Nah, I told him I's working for McAllister now and I's just doin' what I's told."

"Good," The Boss answered as he popped the last nail on the lid of the wooden box. "I'm hoping if the father knows the proof is on its way, maybe he'll wire the money sooner and we can be done with all this." Finally, he removed the lid and looked inside. His lips curled into a smile.

"What is it?" Rusty asked.

The Boss turned toward the other men and held up a plate for show. It was a piece from the set of china Mrs. Coventry had so proudly shown Jacob.

"We're gonna make a killin' by the time we're through here, boys."

The larger man arched his back and laughed. "All cuz the man couldn't hold his liquor!"

At that, the hired hands faced each other, hooked arms, and began skipping around in a circle. They laughed and cheered and started humming to what sounded like "Skip to My Lou."

"Come on, now!" The Boss barked. "Help me get this stuff inside."

They each grabbed something off the back and headed toward the house.

"How ya gonna explain where this here stuff went?" the larger man asked.

"That's easy, Hewey. I'll blame the kid I put in charge of loading everything up." Jacob's teeth clenched so tight his jaw began to hurt.

A moment later Rusty stepped back outside. "These trunks too?"

The Boss followed close behind. "Nah, I'll take them to McAllister's."

And there it was, straight from the horse's mouth. The Boss and Declan McAllister were not one in the same.

The hired hands closed the trunk and loaded it back onto the wagon. Then they led the horses with the wagon attached into the old barn.

Jacob's pulse raced.

The Boss was alone.

Hands twitching at his sides, Jacob wanted so badly to take him down. But, armed with only a pocket-knife, even one on one, he couldn't chance it. His best option was to wait for them to fall asleep and get himself back to town. Sheriff Walker would know what to do.

Jacob released a frustrated breath, looked up at the moon, and settled in for a long wait.

Chapter Thirteen

Sometime early Sunday morning

Jacob startled awake. The moon had jumped across the sky. He cursed himself, he hadn't meant to fall asleep.

All was quiet, save for a low occasional rumble.

Jacob got to his knees and peeked out.

Orange coals were all that was left of their fire and he saw at least two lumps laying nearby. Jacob realized then that the noise he was hearing was snoring.

From this vantage point, Jacob couldn't be sure where the third man was. He assumed somewhere not far away, passed out drunk like his buddies.

Moving slow and careful, he left the safety of his hiding spot and made his way to the barn.

He slid the door open just enough to slip through. It was markedly darker inside, but he noticed a lantern hanging nearby.

Jacob closed the door and lit the lantern. Removing it from the hook, he held it up and turned slowly, taking in his surroundings.

Stalls lined the wall to the left—the first four seemed to be occupied. Tack and saddles hung from pegs and braces along the wall to the right.

Jacob bypassed the saddles, grabbing only a bridle. He needed to get in and out quick.

The horse in the third stall came forward into the light, curious. So Jacob put the lantern down on a nearby barrel and approached.

"Hello there," he whispered, stroking the side of the animal's head. "Are you going to be good for me?"

The horse snorted and huffed, bobbing its head.

Jacob opened the stall door and slid inside. He latched the door behind him and stepped up to the chestnut and white pinto. He ran his hands along its withers and back, then down its flank. He'd worked with horses enough to know it was better to go slow and let the beast know they could trust you.

"So what have we got here?" Jacob asked in a soothing voice as he glanced down below. "A mare," he replied to himself, moving back toward her head. "You are a beauty."

Lifting the bridle, Jacob slipped the bit into her mouth and popped the crown over her ears. He was working the buckle, when a voice came out of nowhere.

"Is that you, Rusty?"

In an instant, Jacob crouched out of sight and peeked between the slats separating the stalls. The Boss stood alone in the open doorway.

Jacob held his breath and took a moment to work up the courage for what he was about to do.

Finally, he swallowed hard and groaned.

"Yeah," he answered in a voice deeper than his own as he moved toward the back of the stall, putting the horse between him and the open aisle. "Just checkin' on the horses. They was stirrin' an' I thought maybe a wild critter got in or somethin'."

"Did ya find anything?"

"Nah. All's good. I got it." Jacob released a calming breath and prayed it worked.

He remained still, waiting in the silence.

After a few seconds, he heard feet shuffling on the dry ground. He peeked through the slats again. But The Boss hadn't moved. The sound had come from someone else approaching.

Rusty, of all people.

The men looked at each other with confusion—The Boss more so. He lifted a finger to his lips, warning Rusty not to speak. Then he pointed in Jacob's direction.

Rusty gave a nod and disappeared. Surely, his plan was to surround the threat.

Jacob shrunk to the floor of the dark stall. Feeling defeated, he squeezed his eyes shut and knocked the back of his head slowly, silently, against the slatted wall behind him.

But he knew he couldn't give up without a fight.

Especially since it wasn't only his life that was in danger.

He heard the way those men talked about Tillie. He heard their disgusting thoughts. Their plans. And he would do everything in his power to stop them. Tillie was the reason he was in his current predicament after all.

Just the thought of one of them putting a hand on her, brought on a new energy. It gave him strength. Fueled his rage. His jaw clamped, and lips parted as he bared his teeth in a silent growl.

Jacob scanned the area for anything he could use as a weapon. There were plenty of things he could use on the wall across the aisle. He just couldn't get to them. Then he noticed what looked like a handle through the slats to the next stall down.

Moving swiftly and carefully, Jacob made his way to the other side of the stall. On his hands and knees, he lowered himself closer to the floor and peered through the bottom slat. A pitchfork.

He'd found himself a pitchfork!

It took some finagling and finesse, but Jacob managed to get ahold of it. Then he hid in the hay pile that sat in the front corner, adjacent to the stall door. He laid the pitchfork down, tucking the long handle and prongs flat against the front wall. A water bucket that hung between him and the door, provided even more coverage.

If Jacob were lucky, the men would stay in the aisle, not see him, and move on. And if he weren't so lucky, he was in the position to ambush. Surprise would be his main defense.

While his pulse raced, Jacob tried to keep his breathing slow and steady. His view was limited to just the area in front of the stall—about fifteen feet wide and not much higher than the knees. But that was enough.

So far, he heard only one set of boots on the wood floor of the barn. They came from the front. The steps were slow and methodical. And they didn't seem to wander. Jacob pictured The Boss's movement.

Step. Together. Inspect. Step. Together. Inspect.

That boded well for Jacob.

Finally, The Boss's feet came into view.

Jacob held his breath.

Step. Together. Inspect. Step. Together. Inspect...
Turn.

Jacob's heart slammed against his ribs. He slowly turned his head to watch the stall door.

Click, went the latch.

And that's when it hit him.

Jacob's gaze panned to the right, toward the front legs of the horse and the reins dangling in front of them. It was the bridle that had given him away.

The stall door opened, washing the immediate area in light. Broken only by The Boss's shadow. He stood still and cautious for several moments before taking his first step. The barrel of his gun crossed the threshold first, followed by one foot and then another.

The Boss stilled just inside the stall. With his eyes straight ahead, he focused on the dark corners in the back. He bent at the waist and peered around and under the mare, then straightened and slowly extended his right leg forward to take another step.

With both hands on the handle, Jacob thrust the pitchfork at The Boss's lower legs. The wide prongs wedged around his back one. Then in quick succession, Jacob jerked, twisted, and lifted the pitchfork, causing the man to fall backward.

The Boss's gun shot off toward the ceiling as his feet left the ground.

From inside the stall, Jacob watched as the man landed flat on his back, the momentum propelling his right arm over his head and finally slamming to the ground and knocking the gun free.

Jacob rushed out.

The Boss lay writhing on the ground in the middle of the aisle, the pitchfork still tangled in his legs. Though, judging by his ragged gasps and the way he clutched his side, it was his lack of air that seemed to distress him most. He'd likely broken a rib or two in the fall.

Jacob pulled the pitchfork free and stood over the man. Blood dotted his pants where one of the prongs had pierced the skin.

A noise from the back of the barn alerted Jacob. He quickly positioned the pitchfork over The Boss's chest and looked into the shadows.

Rusty stepped from behind the wagon and into the light, gun drawn.

"Put the gun on the floor and kick it away," Jacob ordered. He cocked his head and jerked the pitchfork. "Do it or I'll kill him!"

Rusty's narrowed eyes never left Jacob as he lowered the gun to the ground and kicked it toward the wall.

"Wait a minute," Rusty said as his expression softened with realization. "I know who you are. Yer that kid from the poker game … the one who cheated."

Jacob looked down into The Boss's eyes. Seeing the man finally put the connection together amused him. The fact that Jacob currently had the upper hand, also amused him.

"Is that what all this is about?" The Boss asked breathlessly.

Shaking his head, Jacob sneered. "I honestly don't care about the money you stole from me."

Jacob sensed movement in his peripheral. He pressed the prongs to the man's chest and eyed Rusty.

"Don't take another step!"

Rusty held his hands up and eased back.

Jacob addressed The Boss again. "This is about Mathilda Coventry and the fact that I know you're an imposter." The man wrinkled his brow. "That's right … I don't know where the real Declan McAllister is, but I know it ain't you and I know about your plans—"

Jacob never saw it coming, Rusty slamming him with his body.

The two stumbled over The Boss and tumbled to the

ground. They wrestled and rolled, each fighting for dominance.

Finally, Jacob got to his feet. He shuffled from side to side, fists up and to the ready.

Rusty did the same.

And the dance continued.

But evenly matched, neither gained much ground. For every punch that landed, at least one would miss.

Jacob delivered a teeth-breaking blow to Rusty's jaw. But then he took a painful hit to the cheekbone. Swelling quickly began to hinder Jacob's sight, giving him a disadvantage as he tried to keep one eye on The Boss.

One moment The Boss hadn't moved and in the next, he had rolled to his stomach.

Jacob blocked another blow and glanced at The Boss again. He was now on his knees.

As Jacob brought his gaze back to Rusty, he glimpsed the bucket end of a shovel swinging toward his head. Jacob quickly ducked. He felt the breeze as it passed inches above him.

Jacob righted himself and stepped back. His foot bumped something, and he looked down. It was the pitchfork he'd dropped when Rusty tackled him. He bent to grab it as Rusty came at him again with the shovel.

While Rusty swung high, Jacob picked up the pitchfork and swung low. Then, thrusting up with the blunt side, he got the other man in his most sensitive area. Between the legs.

Rusty instantly dropped the shovel. Bending at the waist, his hands covered his privates as he let out a high-pitched moan.

Jacob struck again with an upward motion, using the face of the iron prongs to deliver a blow to the man's chin.

Rusty's head flew back. His body followed and he landed in a lump on the ground.

Jacob's head snapped to The Boss. He was on his feet, stumbling toward a gun.

Jacob dropped the pitchfork and ran. Springing forward, he dove for the weapon.

The Boss dove too.

Both had a hand on it as they grappled on the ground. But neither actually had control of it.

Until finally one of them did…

With one arm clutching his ribs and the other slack at his side, The Boss staggered to his feet. He hovered over Jacob, teetering, and not able to stand completely upright. Then he took a raspy breath and slowly raised his arm, taking aim.

Jacob could tell by the way the man blinked and stared, that he was having a hard time focusing. So, he used that to his advantage.

Keeping his head down and to the side, Jacob sprung from the ground and launched himself at the other man. Jacob's shoulder took the brunt of it, colliding with The Boss's abdomen as he locked his arms around him and propelled him backward.

As the two once again tussled, they tripped over a bucket, knocked tools from the wall, and crashed into a wooden barrel.

It was the sound of broken glass that finally brought the struggle to a pause.

For one brief moment, the men directed their attention to the shattered lantern above all else. Watching in horror as the flame walked across the barn floor, quickly growing and splitting and igniting everything in its path. A path that was quickly separating the two men from the exit at the front.

On the other side of the flames, Jacob saw Rusty pull himself to his feet and run out of the barn.

Then behind Jacob, The Boss began to scream.

Jacob's head snapped in his direction.

Flames crept up the back of The Boss's coat. Arms flailing in the air, the man tried to wriggle free before the fire consumed him.

Bile gurgled in Jacob's throat as he looked away.

He couldn't help him.

But he could still help the horses.

He ran to the farthest stall and whipped open the door. Running inside, he slapped the horse on the hindquarters.

"Go on," he yelled. "Get out of here!"

Then he did the same with the first and second stall, before working his way back to the third.

He had to hurry. It wouldn't be long before fire would completely cut off his exit.

Jacob threw the door open and rushed in. Swinging the reins over the mare's head, Jacob grabbed a fistful of her mane, kicked his leg up, and mounted her bare back.

Just one kick of his heels and the mare bolted from the stall.

Flames ran up the walls, licking the rafters. How long before the roof would start to cave in?

The sounds of crackling and popping, along with the intense roar of the fire were overwhelming. But not as much as the heat. Jacob had never been so afraid in his life.

Leaning forward, Jacob pressed his body close to the horse's back and covered his head with one arm.

"Come on, girl," he cried. "Get us out of here!"

Chapter Fourteen

Sunday, 9:00 a.m.

The walk to church was a short one from the hotel.

Tillie was a bit surprised by the number of people in the streets. They came from all directions, traveling toward the same destination. Parents walked arm in arm, as children laughed and played, usually several steps ahead. Friends and neighbors greeted each other merrily and joined as one in the street. Colorado Springs seemed a tightknit community and the people seemed happy.

That's all Tillie wanted. And if this was where she had to live, she was okay with that. But she needed more than a place to make her happy. She needed a husband to love and cherish her.

Unfortunately, she didn't think Declan McAllister had it in him.

They were to meet Declan at the church. Tillie wondered which of his personalities would show up today. Would he be indifferent and sketchy, like the man she met the first day? Or maybe jealous and arrogant, like he was last night? Of course, she hoped for the charming and personable man she'd glimpsed at dinner.

"Hello Coventry family," Mr. Salzman said with a big smile as they approached the front steps of the church.

"Hello there, Edgar," her father greeted, reaching out and shaking the other man's hand. "Beautiful morning, wouldn't you say?"

"That it is." The hotel owner gestured to the woman beside him. "You remember my lady friend, Mavis Mumford?"

"Yes, of course. Good morning to you, Ms. Mumford."

"Good morning," she replied, smiling, and nodding to each in turn. "We were just about to go in and take our seats. Won't you join us?"

"If you're sure there's room for four," her father answered. "Mathilda's fiancé will be joining us, as well."

"We always make room for friends," Mr. Salzman said, slapping Tillie's father on the shoulder.

The Coventry family followed Mr. Salzman and his lady friend into the church, which was already beginning to fill. They found a pew with enough room to fit six and slid in from the center, leaving an empty seat near the aisle for Declan.

Before long, the church was packed. Every seat taken save for the one next to Tillie. The one she'd held and explained several times "was saved for someone."

As the church doors closed and the room hushed, Tillie looked over her shoulder again.

Where is he?

She felt guilty when she noticed the line of people standing along the back wall.

Tillie's gaze fell on Maggie and her mother, Millie, sitting a few rows back. Maggie smiled and waved.

Tillie waved back.

"Good morning, friends," a robust voice from the front said.

Tillie faced forward as everyone replied "good morning" in unison.

Later, as the Reverend said his final words, Tillie glanced over her shoulder, wondering if Declan had slipped in late during the service and stayed near the back.

He hadn't.

People stood and began filing out of the pews.

Tillie shuffled along with the crowd.

"I wonder what could've happened to him?" her mother whispered to her father.

"I don't know, Dorothy. Maybe he wasn't feeling well."

"You don't suppose he's starting to have second thoughts, do you?"

Is it a sin to wish such a thing while inside a church? Tillie wondered.

"Hi Tillie!" Maggie greeted. She stood at the end of her pew and joined Tillie's side as she approached.

"It's nice to see a familiar face." Tillie smiled.

They stepped out the door, down the steps, and moved to the side.

Maggie looked over Tillie's shoulder. "Is that your father?" she asked.

Tillie followed Maggie's gaze. "Yes."

"Where's your fiancé?"

Before she could answer, another friendly face approached.

"How did it go, yesterday?" Mrs. O'Brien asked, with a raised brow and an optimistic smile.

Tillie shrugged. "Um, okay, I guess." She feared her own smile was less optimistic.

Mrs. O'Brien looked around. "Is he here wit you?"

Now Tillie had both lady's eyes on her, waiting for an answer. She felt her cheeks flush with embarrassment.

"No." She didn't feel comfortable elaborating or speculating at this point in time.

She turned her attention to her parents, who'd stopped to chat with another couple staying at the hotel.

Mr. Salzman and Ms. Mumford walked arm and arm through the crowd of people milling about.

The hotel owner gave a nod and smiled. "Good day, Miss."

Tillie was smiling in return when another man rushed up and grabbed Mr. Salzman's arm, stopping him.

"Excuse me, Edgar. Can I have a moment?"

"Of course. Good to see you, Nathaniel," Mr. Salzman answered.

"You as well."

Tillie turned her attention back to Maggie and Mrs. O'Brien. "So, what does everyone do after church around here?" She was hoping for an invite of some sort. She'd love to get more acquainted with the ladies of the Springs.

But then something the other man said to Mr. Salzman grabbed her attention.

Her head snapped and demanding eyes fell on the man. "What did you say?"

The man lowered his brow, taken aback by her forward interest.

"Jacob didn't come home last night," he repeated with hesitation.

The hotel owner chimed in with an introduction.

"This is Miss Coventry, a guest at the hotel." Then to her, he said, "Miss Coventry this is Nathaniel Price. Jacob lives and works on Nathaniel's ranch." Tillie couldn't help but notice the concerned—almost pained—look on Mr. Salzman's normally cheery face.

And while she had her own worries involving Jacob's whereabouts, she wondered what the hotel owner knew.

She wasn't the only one who noticed something was amiss.

"What is it, Edgar?" Nathaniel prodded impatiently.

Mr. Salzman raised his chin, passing a glance over Tillie, then landing on Nathaniel. "I sure hope he didn't do anything stupid."

He knows something. "Did Jacob talk to you last night?" Tillie asked.

"He did."

Tillie gasped as another thought crossed her mind. *Last night Jacob disappeared the same time Declan left the hotel.* "You don't think he'd go after Declan and confront him, do you?"

"I've heard enough," Nathaniel said. "I'm getting Sheriff Walker."

Mr. Salzman watched as Nathaniel cut through the crowd. Then he took off after him.

Tillie felt like she couldn't catch her breath. Her knees wobbled and she grabbed the arm closest to her.

Mrs. O'Brien helped steady Tillie, wrapping an arm around her. "Don't worry, dear. I'm sure yer Mr. McAllister is goin' t'be just fine."

Tillie knew the kind woman was only trying to comfort her. But, in fact, the woman's words tore at her heart. Because it wasn't her fiancé she was worried about.

It was Jacob.

"Tillie," her mother cried, rushing to her side. "What happened? You're white as a ghost."

Mrs. O'Brien answered before Tillie could. "I'm not

sure, somethin' to do wit someone named Jacob and Mr. McAllister."

After several minutes, Mr. Salzman returned.

"Nathaniel is going to follow the sheriff out to McAllister's. You can ride out with him and I'll see that his family gets home. Go quickly, he's waiting for you," the hotel owner said waving Tillie and her parents toward Nathaniel's wagon.

THE RIDE to Declan's was quick. And quiet.

Tillie's mind raced with possibilities and scenarios— none of them ending well.

As the wagon approached, the first thing Tillie noticed was the horse in the corral. Yesterday, there were three.

Since the sheriff had beat them by a few minutes, he was coming out of the house as the wagon came to a stop.

"No one's inside," he said as he left the porch and headed for the gate.

"Two of his horses seem to be gone," Tillie replied.

"Nathaniel, check the barn," Sheriff Walker ordered. "See if his wagon is here or if there's any sign of Jacob."

"You got it, Jim," Nathaniel said as he jumped down from the wagon.

"I'm going to check the outhouse and around back," the sheriff added.

Tillie decided to check inside the house to see if anything looked out of place since she was there the day before. Meanwhile, her parents stayed near the wagon.

At first glance, everything looked the same. But Tillie had a feeling she was missing something.

As she stood in the doorway between the kitchen and the sitting room, pondering the space, she could hear various shouts coming from outside.

"Hello! Is anyone here?"

"Declan!"

"Jacob?"

Suddenly it occurred to Tillie what was missing. She ran up the stairs and checked the rooms up there. But the two rooms were just as bare as the first floor.

Where were all her things?

Declan had left the hotel last night with two large trunks and several smaller packages.

Tillie ran out the door and spotted Nathaniel in the barn opening. Hands on his hips, his eyes wandered over the surrounding land.

"Is his wagon here?" Tillie called out at the top of her voice.

"No," he answered.

"How about a couple of trunks and some other baggage? Do you see anything like that?"

Rotating at his waist, Nathaniel looked back and forward again. "Nope!"

But before Tillie had a chance to process what that could mean, the sheriff shouting in the distance caught everyone's attention.

"I've got a body back here!"

Chapter Fifteen

____

Sunday 10:10 a.m.

Tillie's heart sank.

A body?

Nathaniel and her father took off running in the direction of the sheriff's voice.

Tillie ran to her mother's arms. Then, together, the shaken women trailed behind.

Squatting next to a small mound on the other side of a neglected vegetable garden behind the house, Sheriff Walker looked up, his face grim. "It's McAllister."

Despite the warm sun overhead, a shiver ran down Tillie's spine. No matter what she thought of the man, she'd never wish him—or anybody, for that matter—dead.

And what of Jacob?

How could he do this?

How could she ever face him again?

While Nathaniel sidled up to the sheriff and looked into the shallow grave, Tillie's father stayed back a good ten to fifteen feet. He spread his arms, protectively, shielding the women's view.

"Are you sure it's Declan McAllister?" he asked.

"Yep," the sheriff answered. He shook his head and rubbed the back of his neck.

Tillie buried her face in her mother's embrace.

"Dear God," her mother whispered, stroking Tillie's back.

"Didn't you say you were with McAllister last night?" the sheriff asked.

"Yes," her father answered. "He had dinner with us at the hotel."

Sheriff Walker grunted.

"What is it, Sheriff?"

"It's just that … it looks like he's been here a while," the sheriff added.

"What do you mean, a while?"

"Uh, I don't know." The sheriff cocked his head as he looked into the ground again. "At least a month, I'd say."

Tillie raised her chin. Holding her breath, she stepped out of her mother's arms.

Her father passed a concerned look to her and her mother. "Stay here."

The women watched as he stepped up to the grave and looked in. He silently stared for what seemed like a lifetime.

"Well, Teddy? Is it Declan?" Her mother's voice shook.

Finally, he met their gaze.

"I don't know how to say this," he replied with hesitation, confusion contorting his face.

"Just say it!" her mother prodded.

Tillie's father met the sheriff's gaze. He pointed toward the body in the ground. "If *this* is Declan McAllister …

then who have we been talking to since we arrived in Colorado Springs?"

"What!" Her mother's face blanched with shock and dismay. "I have to see this for myself," she announced, marching toward the others.

Meanwhile, Tillie shut out the world around her, escaping into her thoughts and wandering back toward the front of the house.

Tillie replayed yesterday's visit, picking apart all the inconsistencies and clues.

Then she went through her conversation with Jacob.

He tried to warn me.

He said Declan wasn't who he said he was.

She thought he meant figuratively.

"Tillie, what is it?" her father touched her arm. "You looked like you were deep in thought."

That, she was. So much so that she hadn't noticed everyone standing around her. Staring at her like she had the answers.

Maybe she did.

Tillie eyed Sheriff Walker. "Does the name Reed Larson mean anything to you?"

His brow dipped instantly. "Yeah. Where'd you hear that name?"

"Who's Reed Larson?" her father demanded, eyes darting between his daughter and the sheriff.

"They call him *The Boss* the sheriff answered. "He's bad news. Wanted in at least four states."

Tillie met her mother's gaze, and they shared a look of understanding. The puzzle was coming together.

"Tillie found a quit claim deed with the name Reed Larson on it. Mr. McAllister had signed this property over to him," her mother explained, somberly. "It was dated about a month ago."

"Why didn't anyone tell me about this?" her father barked angrily.

"We were going to. We just hadn't had a chance yet. Tillie showed it to me last night while you and Declan—or whoever he is—were helping load up the wagon."

"Jacob!" Tillie gasped. She'd been so focused on the body and the possible killer, that she almost forgot to tell them. "We have to find him. Last night he tried to warn me. He suspected Declan wasn't who he said he was, and I didn't believe him." Her breath hitched as tears welled in her eyes.

"It's okay," her mother said, wrapping an arm around Tillie in an attempt to calm her.

"No, you don't understand!" Growing angry, Tillie shrugged free. Her voice quivered as she began to sob. "It's my fault. I told him unless he had actual proof, I had to marry Declan.

"Don't you see? Jacob went after this dangerous man, I know it!" she cried. "And because of me he could be out there somewhere hurt or … dead!"

Sheriff Walker stepped forward. "Don't you worry, miss. We'll find him."

"What are ya thinking, Jim?" Nathaniel asked. "Got any ideas where this Larson guy might be hanging out?"

Sheriff Walker put his hands on his hips and scanned the horizon. "My guess is he's been hanging out in Colorado City. I know he's a big gambler, we'll have to check all the saloons…"

That triggered a memory.

Mrs. O'Brien had told Tillie that Declan—the real Declan—had gotten himself into trouble in a saloon in Colorado City.

She tuned into the conversation again as the sheriff was saying, "…and with the amount of miners that travel through there it would be pretty easy for a guy like him to blend in."

"The Good Luck Saloon," Tillie blurted. All eyes turned to her. "I think that's where Declan may have met Reed Larson."

The sheriff's brow rose in surprise. "Alrighty then." He turned, gesturing for Nathaniel to follow. "Let's go!"

Nathaniel started toward his wagon.

"We're coming too," Tillie demanded.

And without question, her parents followed.

WITH SHERIFF WALKER on his horse and the rest of them in the wagon, they all traveled together back down the road that ran parallel to the creek. Though this time, they turned away from Colorado Springs and crossed the bridge toward Colorado City.

Tillie's father sat on the driver's bench with Nathaniel, while she and her mother sat at the rear of the wagon, their feet dangling off the back.

The hardpacked road headed west, straight for the mountains. Being that it was still early in the day, Tillie kept her chin down and a hand to her forehead, to shield her eyes from the glare of the sun.

Eventually the wagon rounded a bend and headed north, alongside the base of the Rockies.

With the change in direction, Tillie dropped her hand and let her gaze wander the landscape to the south.

She noticed a dark figure in the distance.

"What is that?" she asked her mother.

Following Tillie's gaze, her mother let out an inquisitive grunt. "Huh, it looks like a horse."

"It looks too big to be a horse, but it does look like its

moving." Something didn't feel right about whatever it was Tillie was looking at. She called out to Nathaniel. "Can we turn around and check something?"

"What is it?"

"There's something back there, the other way," she said, pointing.

"Whoa." Nathaniel brought the horses to a stop and turned in his seat.

"Why ya stoppin'?" the sheriff asked, steering his horse closer to the wagon.

Tillie climbed to her feet. Standing in the bed of the wagon, she hoped for a better perspective.

"What is that?" she asked, watching the dark figure as it moved slowly in their direction.

"What the—" Sheriff Walker gave a kick, and his horse took off.

"Hold on," Nathaniel ordered.

Tillie rush to the front of the wagon bed and gripped the bench back. And with that, Nathaniel tapped the reins and brought the wagon about.

As they moved closer, it became clear that the dark figure was in fact a horse. But it was carrying something on its back.

It wasn't until they were well upon it that they realized it wasn't a *something*, it was a *someone.* The rider lie on his stomach, straddling the horse's back. His legs and arms hanging loose down the sides.

Sheriff Walker got there first. He slowly eased his horse up next to the other horse, so as not to spook it. Then he reached for the loose reins and jumped to the ground.

"It's Jacob," the sheriff announced as the wagon pulled to a stop. "Help me get him down!"

Nathaniel leapt from the wagon.

Tillie did the same, rushing up beside them as the men carefully pulled Jacob from the horse.

She gasped at the sight of him and covered her mouth with her hand.

Not only were his skin and clothes covered with black soot, but there was a gaping hole across the back of his shirt. It revealed a burn about three inches wide and nearly twelve inches in length.

"Let's put him in the wagon," Nathaniel said. Then to Tillie's mother, he added, "Grab a blanket. There's one rolled up under the bench."

Jacob's body hung limp, his head lolling back, as the men carried him by his arms and legs. One eye was swollen, his face smeared with blood.

"Is he breathing?" Tillie cried, walking alongside them.

The men didn't answer.

Maybe they didn't know. But Tillie feared they just didn't want to say.

"Get the canteen out of my saddlebag," the sheriff ordered Tillie.

She got the canteen and rushed back.

The men laid Jacob delicately on the wool blanket her mother had laid out and Tillie climbed in beside him. Her mother sat on her knees at the front, near the driver's bench, worry drawing lines in her face.

"Open this," Tillie said, handing her mother the canteen.

While her mother obliged, Tillie lifted her skirt, revealing her petticoat. Then she grabbed the bottom hem of the white undergarment with both hands and tore off a long strip. Wadding up the cloth, she took the canteen and wetted it.

Sheriff Walker hovered at the side of the wagon as Tillie cleaned Jacob's face. As did Nathaniel.

He grabbed Jacob's hand. "Jacob, can you hear me?"
Everyone remained still and quiet.
But Tillie worried it was quiet too long.
"Wake up, Jacob. Please," Tillie cried softly.

Chapter Sixteen

Sunday 10:45

Tillie's face was the first thing Jacob saw when he opened his eyes. She seemed to be glowing and floating over him, like an angel.

But he knew he wasn't dead because his eye hurt like the dickens. And surely if he were in heaven, he would no longer feel pain. That was his assumption, anyway.

Could I be dreaming?

"Sit him up and get him some water."

Jacob turned his head toward the voice and saw Nathaniel's face.

"No way I'm dreaming if *you're* here," Jacob muttered.

Nathaniel's brow dipped. "What?"

Jacob laughed to himself and turned his head and his gaze back to Tillie. He realized now that it was the sun directly behind her that cast the golden light, giving her the ethereal appearance.

He smiled. "That's better."

"Pfft, he's fine," Nathaniel groaned with a light-hearted tone.

And with that everyone else sighed with relief.

With Nathaniel on one side and Tillie on the other, they grabbed his arms and helped him sit up.

A flash of pain brought stars to Jacob's eyes and he sucked in a breath through his teeth.

"Is it your back?" Tillie asked.

Closing his eyes, he slowly blew the breath out.

"Yeah," Jacob finally answered. "Got hit with a beam."

Tillie offered Jacob the canteen. "Do you need help?"

"No, I got it." Jacob lifted the canteen to his lips, threw his head back, and guzzled. He hadn't realized how thirsty he was until it was gone. "Sorry," he said, handing it back empty.

For the first time, Jacob looked around, taking in everyone's faces. He wondered why they were all here … together?

"Can you tell us what happened?" Sheriff Walker asked.

Jacob nodded.

Sheepishly, he met Tillie's gaze.

"You went after him, didn't you?" she asked with sad eyes.

Jacob grimaced.

"I'm sorry. I never meant…" He lowered his gaze.

"I need to say something first," Mr. Coventry began with hesitation. He stood beside the wagon, just over Tillie's shoulder.

Tensing, Jacob prepared himself for disappointment. Would anyone believe him? Or would he be held responsible for ruining Tillie's wedding? And worse, for the fire and the death of another man?

Mr. Coventry cleared his throat and began again,

"Don't worry, son. Whatever happened, you did it to protect my daughter … and for that, I owe you my life."

Jacob's mouth opened, and then closed. His eyes shifted to Tillie. "I don't understand."

"We found the body of the real Declan McAllister this morning," she said.

Sheriff Walker chimed in. "It's likely the man posing as McAllister is Reed Larson. He's a card sharp and a confidence man who's wanted in at least four states for swindling lots of folks and killing anyone who gets in his way. He usually travels with two guys who do most the dirty work. They call him—"

"The Boss," Jacob said, finishing the sheriff's sentence.

"Yeah," Sheriff Walker confirmed.

"I don't think he'll be hurting anyone ever again." Jacob lowered his head. He'd only meant to get the proof he needed. He never meant to come face to face with the men. And while he knew it was either him or them … he would never want to be responsible for another man's death.

He went on to explain how he'd stowed away in the back of the man's wagon, then stayed hidden and listened to the three of them carry on with their vulgar talk and cheating ways. And how he waited until he thought they'd all passed out drunk before attempting to make his escape.

"But while I was in the barn trying to snatch a horse, The Boss and the red-haired fella, Rusty, found me. There was a scuffle and then a fire broke out … it all happened so fast.

"Rusty was quick to run as soon as the fire started. I'm bettin' he and the other one—I think they called him Hewey—are long gone by now."

"Can you take us there?" The sheriff asked.

• • •

JACOB LED them back to the homestead The Boss and his men had taken over. Wisps of smoke in the sky made it easy to find.

They sat on the small hill overlooking the property. The barn had been reduced to embers and ash, and there was no sign of Rusty or Hewey. Two of the three horses Jacob had set free, grazed in a nearby field.

"I want to have a look inside to be sure no one's home," Sheriff Walker said. "Everyone stay here."

With one hand on the gun in his holster and the other holding the reins, the sheriff slowly rode his horse closer.

"Anyone home?" he called out. When he got no response, he dismounted and went the rest of the way on foot. Standing beside the door, he pulled his weapon and knocked. "Hello! This is Sheriff Walker."

Finally, he opened the door and went inside.

After a minute he reappeared in the doorway and waved the rest of them down.

Nathaniel drove the wagon up to the house.

"Did you say they took some of Miss Coventry's things into the house?" the sheriff asked.

"Yes, they planned on selling what they could," he answered. "Unfortunately, they left the trunks on the wagon and parked it in…" his gaze turned to the smoldering rubble that was the barn.

"Oh no, that's practically your whole wardrobe," Tillie's mother fretted.

Tillie pressed her lips together and sighed. "It's fine, mother."

That was the first Tillie had spoken in a half hour.

Sheriff Walker addressed Tillie's father. "Why don't you go inside and see what you can find of hers. I want to take a look around to make sure they aren't hiding out anywhere or if they left anything behind from previous victims."

Mr. Coventry lowered himself from the wagon.

"I want to come too, Teddy," Mrs. Coventry replied to which her husband helped her to the ground.

"How can I help, Jim?" Nathaniel asked.

"You wanna round up those horses, I hate to leave 'em out here to fend for themselves."

"You got it." Nathaniel engaged the brake and hopped down.

"You can grab rope from my saddle," Sheriff Walker added as Nathaniel walked away. He turned back to Tillie and Jacob sitting in the bed of the wagon. "You two stay here and keep an eye out."

Alone, Jacob faced Tillie. "I'm sorry you lost all your things."

"I'm not," she answered with a shrug. "Those dresses weren't practical for Colorado Springs, anyway."

"Well, now that you don't have to get married, won't you be going back to New York?"

Tillie dropped her eyes to her fidgeting hands in her lap.

"I was thinking that maybe I could stay," she said, looking up through her lashes with a coy smile.

Jacob's lips curled into a huge grin. "I'd like that."

Chapter Seventeen

Monday, 10:00 a.m.

Jacob walked into the Sheriff's office.

Sheriff Walker got up from his chair behind his desk and extended his hand. "Thanks for coming down this morning. How ya feeling? Looks like the swelling has gone down some."

Jacob shook the man's hand. "It has—probably looks worse than it feels. My back is a little tender, but I'll be all right."

"Good, good." The sheriff gestured to a chair in front of the desk. "Have a seat."

Jacob felt sick, deep in the pit of his stomach. The sheriff's small talk worried him.

Was he in trouble with the law?

"So, you're probably wondering why I asked you to come down?"

"Yeah." Jacob swallowed hard.

"I think I mentioned that Reed Larson was a wanted man..."

"Yeah," Jacob repeated, the word curling with skepticism.

"What I didn't mention, was that there was a five-thousand dollar reward out for him … dead or alive—"

"Wait. You're not arresting me?"

"What? No." Sheriff Walker cracked a smile. "Is that what you thought?"

Jacob breathed a sigh of relief, then started laughing.

Sheriff Walker chuckled. He continued, "It'll take about a week for the money to be wired, but I just wanted to let you know."

"Oh boy." Jacob couldn't wipe the smile from his face. "You don't know how much getting this money means to me."

"I'm sure." He smiled again. "Watcha gonna do with it?"

"Fifty of it is going to pay off my debt to Mr. Salzman and the rest is going toward building my own house."

The office door opened, and the men turned their attention.

Mr. Coventry walked in first, then held the door as his wife crossed the threshold. Tillie followed a few feet behind.

Jacob got to his feet and removed his hat.

She smiled the moment their eyes met.

A warm rush washed over Jacob.

He'd gambled with his life and won the money, now it was time to gamble with his heart.

———

TILLIE HELD Jacob's gaze as they entered the Sheriff's office. Even with a black eye, he was so handsome. And the way he looked at her made her feel like her heart was trying to break out of her chest.

She hadn't found a way to tell her parents that she wanted to stay in Colorado, yet. It wasn't that she was having second thoughts, but that she needed to talk to Jacob. She needed to know they had a future.

"Sorry to intrude," her father said as he crossed the room. "But I have that information you asked for on McAllister's next of kin."

Jacob stepped out of the way to let her father approach.

Or maybe it was an excuse to get closer to her?

Tillie felt her cheeks flush.

She subtly eyed him from the side and whispered, "What are you doing here?"

"Talking to the sheriff about Reed Larson," he whispered back.

Her mother stood on the other side of her, so Tillie didn't feel free to say more at the moment.

"Declan's father is a friend of mine," her father was saying to the sheriff. "I sent word of his death this morning." There was a weight to his voice. "I'd like to go out to his property and gather anything of importance that I can take back to his family."

"How very thoughtful," Sheriff Walker replied. "How soon might you be leaving town?"

"Dorothy and I were discussing it this morning," her father said, passing a glance to his wife and then back to the sheriff. Tillie's shoulders tensed. She wasn't aware of any such discussion. "I think we'll leave the day after tomorrow. It's been a rough few days and I think it best we get back home."

Tillie's eyes snapped to Jacob, her brow heavy with worry. She expected to have more time.

But Jacob gazed back at her, serene as ever.

Tillie's head cocked with curiosity and their silent exchange continued.

Slowly, Jacob's lips curled into a smile—a smile that reached his sparkling blue eyes.

He winked. Then looked toward her father.

"Excuse me, Mr. Coventry. I don't mean to interrupt, but I have something I want to say."

Her father turned. "What is it, son?"

Looking down at the floor, Jacob clenched and curled the rim of his hat with both hands. Finally, he took a deep breath and met the man's gaze again. "I don't normally work at the hotel, sir. I'm a ranch hand. I love what I do, and I love the people I work for—"

Her father's brow wrinkled. "Why are you telling me this?"

Tillie wondered the same.

"I could never give your daughter the material things she's used to, but I can promise to love her with everything I've got."

Goose bumps covered Tillie's arms. Tears welled in the corners of her eyes.

"Are you asking for my daughter's hand?"

Jacob met her gaze and smiled. "If she'll have me."

Tillie let the tears spill. Too overwhelmed to speak, she nodded hastily.

Beside her, her mother sobbed. "That was the most beautiful thing I've ever heard." She took a ragged breath and lifted a handkerchief to her face.

Tillie's father took one look at his wife, shook his head, and laughed. "I guess we're still having a wedding."

With that, Jacob threw his arms around Tillie's waist and lifted her off the ground. She wrapped her arms around his neck as he spun wildly in a circle.

"Woohoo!" he cheered as Tillie giggled. "I'm the happiest man this side of the Mississippi."

Jacob set Tillie back on her feet, but he continued to hold her tight and gaze into her eyes. And in that moment, it was as if they were the only two people who existed.

Putting a finger under her chin, Jacob guided her as he brought his lips to hers. They were warm and soft and didn't linger as long as she'd have liked. But she had to remind herself that they were not in fact alone.

It had only been a second, but already she was looking forward to kissing him again. She was looking forward to a lot of things. But most of all, she looked forward to gazing into those beautiful eyes of his … for the rest of her life.

I want to thank you for purchasing and reading this book.

If you enjoyed Jacob's Jackpot, I would really appreciate it if you could leave me a review on Amazon. I love getting feedback from my readers and reviews on Amazon really make a difference.

Thanks so much!

Michele

About the Author

Michele Lindsey lives in upstate New York with her husband, the cutest pup, and two kitty overlords. She is the mother of two young adults and has been an ice-cream scooper, a wedding DJ, a balloon-toting clown, a travel agent and a dental assistant.

Michele also publishes young adult paranormal romance, under the pseudonym M.L. Stoughton. She is a member of RWA (Romance Writers of America) and its local chapter, STAR (Southern Tier Authors of Romance). Her first novel, Pleasantwick, won a gold medal in the 2017 Readers' Favorite Awards and was chosen as the "Official Selection" for Young Adult Fantasy in the 2017 New Apple Summer E-book Awards.

If you want to know more about what she's working on, please visit her website at www.mlstoughton.com or sign up for her email list. http://eepurl.com/b2Qtv5